Her voice shook. 'Alex—please. Don't do this…'

'Do what?' he questioned. 'This?' He stroked her hair aside, and kissed the nape of her neck. 'Or this?' He bent his head and pressed his lips to Louise's bare shoulder, forcing a shiver of response from her.

'Because I hear what you're saying, my reluctant wife,' he told her softly. 'But all evening I've seen your eyes. Felt the way you've touched me—how you went into my arms. And you know it's true…'

Sara Craven was born in South Devon, and grew up surrounded by books, in a house by the sea. After leaving grammar school she worked as a local journalist, covering everything from flower shows to murders. She started writing for Mills & Boon® in 1975. Apart from writing, her passions include films, music, cooking and eating in good restaurants. She now lives in Somerset.

Sara Craven has appeared as a contestant on the Channel Four game show *Fifteen to One* and is also the latest (and last ever) winner of the *Mastermind of Great Britain* championship.

Recent titles by the same author:

THE MARRIAGE TRUCE
THE FORCED MARRIAGE
HIS CONVENIENT MARRIAGE

THE TOKEN WIFE

BY

SARA CRAVEN

MILLS & BOON®

MILLS & BOON and MILLS & BOON with the Rose Device are registered trademarks of the publisher.

First published in Great Britain 2003
Harlequin Mills & Boon Limited,
Eton House, 18-24 Paradise Road, Richmond, Surrey TW9 1SR

© Sara Craven 2003

ISBN 0 263 83238 4

Set in Times Roman 10 on 11 pt.
01-0603-55717

Printed and bound in Spain
by Litografía Rosés, S.A., Barcelona

PROLOGUE

WHEN Alex Fabian was displeased, his annoyance invariably radiated from him like static electricity, alerting the wary to keep their distance.

Tonight, entering his grandmother's Holland Park house, he was crackling like an approaching storm, although he managed a brief smile for the elderly manservant who admitted him, and who'd known him since childhood.

'Barney—you're well? And Mrs Barnes?'

'Both fighting fit, thank you, Mr Alex.' Barnes paused. 'Her ladyship hasn't come downstairs yet, but you'll find Mr Fabian in the drawing room.'

'My father?' Alex's brows snapped together. 'I thought they weren't speaking to each other.'

'There has been a rapprochement, sir.' Barnes' tone was sedate. 'Last week.'

'I see.' Alex shrugged off his overcoat, and cast a fleeting but critical glance at his reflection in the big gilt-framed mirror before crossing the wide hall to the double doors which led into the drawing room.

He supposed he should have fitted in a visit to the barber, he thought, raking an irritable hand through the tawny hair which brushed his collar.

But the charcoal suit he was wearing, set off by a silk waistcoat in a paler shade of grey, the pristine white shirt, and discreetly striped tie acknowledged that this was a formal visit.

That he'd been sent for.

And his tight-lipped expression and smouldering green eyes indicated that he suspected what was behind the summons.

He found George Fabian seated on one of the sofas that flanked the fireplace, glancing through a newspaper.

He said, without looking up, 'Good evening, Alex. We have been instructed to help ourselves to a drink.'

'Thank you, sir, but it's a little early for me.' Alex glanced pointedly at his watch. 'I wasn't sure whether I was being invited for dinner, or nursery tea.'

'I suggest you ask your grandmother that,' his father advised curtly. 'This little family gathering was her idea, not mine.'

'And its purpose?' Alex walked to the hearth and gave the logs that burned there an impatient kick with a well-shod foot.

'I understand to discuss the arrangements for her birthday party.' George Fabian paused. 'Among other things.'

'Indeed?' Alex's brows rose sardonically. 'And am I permitted to speculate what those "other things" might be?'

His father gave him a dry look. 'I imagine your position as chairman in waiting at Perrins Bank might come up for discussion.'

There was a silence, then Alex said, with a touch of hauteur, 'Are you implying that it could be in some doubt? I wasn't aware that my ability to run the bank was being called into question.'

'It isn't, as far as I know.' George Fabian folded the paper, and tossed it aside. 'It's more a matter of image.' He pursed his lips meditatively. 'Too many pictures in the wrong sort of paper. Too many pieces in the gossip columns. And too many girls,' he added flatly.

'I wasn't aware that I required a vow of celibacy to work at Perrins.' Alex kept his tone light, but his fingers beat a restless tattoo on the edge of the mantelpiece. The fact that he'd been expecting this made it no less unwelcome, he thought, his edginess increasing.

'Then think again,' his father said brusquely. 'Perrins is an old-fashioned bank, run by conservative people, and they don't like the kind of adverse publicity you've been attracting.'

He shook his head. 'The customers want to know that there's someone solid and reliable at the top, whom they can trust. Not a playboy.' He paused. 'You're a high-flyer, Alex, but you're getting perilously close to the sun. Take care you don't come crashing down.'

'Thank you,' Alex said with dangerous politeness. 'Have you been asked to pass on these words of wisdom, or was it all your own work?'

George Fabian sighed wearily. 'Don't be so damned prickly, boy. I'm your father, so I think I have the right to be concerned. I don't want to see you throw away the potential for a brilliant career.'

'If the worst happens, there are other banks besides Perrins,' Alex said tautly.

'Indeed there are,' his father agreed. He gave the younger man a long, steady look. 'Unless, of course, you become too hot for any of them to handle.'

There was a silence, then Alex said quietly, 'Maybe I will have that drink after all.' He went over to the side-table, where decanters and glasses were set out, pouring himself a single malt whisky. 'So.' He turned back, glass in hand, his expression challenging. 'What's the rumour on the piazza?'

'This and that.' Mr Fabian paused. 'I gather Peter Crosby is going to be promoted in the next government reshuffle,' he added almost inconsequentially.

Alex stiffened. 'And?'

'And that means he'll become of increasing interest to the tabloids.'

George Fabian drank some of his own whisky. 'I gather the *Daily Mercury* is already on red alert. And that a news team has been detailed to keep a close eye on his wife.'

There was another, longer silence. Then, 'I see,' said Alex, his voice expressionless.

'In addition,' Mr Fabian went on, 'there's an unconfirmed report that Crosby has consulted a lawyer, and is considering hiring a private detective to follow Mrs Crosby, and monitor her calls.

'There are no children, of course, and he may be preparing to dump the beautiful Lucinda before she jeopardises his triumphant march to power by some further indiscretion. You're not the first, you know.'

'I am aware of that.' Alex's look and tone were icy.

'And it's by no means certain he would go for a simple, no-fault divorce. He has the reputation of being a vindictive bastard.' He gave his son another steady look. 'He could decide to name and shame.'

'It's a pity the bloody gossip-mongers haven't something better to do.' Alex threw the whisky down his throat with a jerky movement.

'They have their uses,' his father returned placidly. 'Perhaps you should be grateful to them. Featuring in a messy, high-profile divorce is something that the Perrins board would never stand for in their chairman.'

Alex's smile glittered. 'Gratitude is not my overriding emotion at the moment.'

George Fabian looked concerned. 'I hope you're not going to tell me that Lucinda Crosby is the love of your life.'

'Certainly not.' His son gave a cynical shrug. 'I doubt if such a creature exists.' He'd been thoroughly enjoying his liaison with Cindy Crosby who was not only beautiful but also sexually voracious, he thought with an inward grimace. But he'd been planning to end it anyway, married women not being entirely to his taste.

He gave his father a stony look. 'I hope that reassures you.'

'Don't congratulate yourself too soon,' Mr Fabian cautioned. 'You're not out of the woods yet.' He paused. 'Have you ever heard your grandmother talk about a cousin of hers who went off to South Africa just before the war—Archie Maidstone?'

Alex frowned. 'Yes, she's mentioned him. I got the impression she'd been very fond of him at one time, and then he got himself into some kind of trouble, and had to be shunted out of the country.'

'That's the one.' George Fabian nodded. 'He had a job with Perrins, and embezzled some money. The family closed ranks and made good the loss, apparently, but he was warned never to come back to England.'

'And has he?' Alex gave a faint whistle. 'He must be a hell of an age.'

'Actually, he's dead,' said Mr Fabian. 'But his grandson isn't, and he's been over here visiting. Building bridges. Seems to have made an excellent impression on your grandmother, too.' He paused. 'He even got her to invite him down to Rosshampton for the weekend.'

Alex's attention was suddenly, sharply focused. 'Go on.'

'He's married,' said George Fabian. 'And she's asked him to come back for her birthday, and bring his wife so that he can show her Rosshampton too.'

Alex went on staring at him. 'Meaning?'

'Just that your inheritance may not be as secure as you thought,' his father said bluntly. 'There's an alternative claimant.'

'I'm her only grandson,' Alex said. 'What is this guy —a second...third cousin? And she's always said that Rosshampton will ultimately come to me. You really think that's in doubt?'

'I don't know,' George Fabian admitted. 'But she's very taken with him—and the fact that he's married...stable. She likes that—and she may have been drawing a few unfavourable comparisons.'

Alex's mouth had firmed into a steely straight line. 'I see.' He glanced up at the picture on the wall above him, a watercolour that he had commissioned for Lady Perrin's eightieth birthday. He saw the elegant grey stone house sheltering among the ancient trees; the sunlight falling in swathes across the sweeping lawns, and, in the distance, the gleam of water.

He thought, with a pang, of how many of the happiest weeks of his childhood had been spent there. How, over the years, it unerringly drew him back to its rock-like security. How it had always seemed enshrined in his heart, timeless and unchanging, waiting for him to become its master.

And his grandmother had encouraged that, he thought with a pang of disquiet. Had deliberately fostered his love for the house, and let him think that it would one day be his.

And now, for the first time, there was a doubt in his mind. A shadow in the sunlight that disturbed him perhaps more than any of the other unpalatable things that had been said to him tonight.

This unknown South African, he thought, his hand tightening round his empty glass. This grandson of a man who'd been sent away in disgrace, but for whom Selina Perrin might cherish tender memories. This man was going to steal Rosshampton from him? Over his dead body!

Then the door opened, and Lady Perrin came in. She was wearing one of the elegant long black dresses she favoured for the evening, and her snowy hair was piled on top of her head in an imperious knot.

Alex saw that she was using the silver-topped cane she usually despised as a sign of weakness, and realised that she must be in real pain from her arthritis to give way like that. The anger and unease within him was replaced by a swift compassion he dared not show.

His father received a brief inclination of the head, and, 'Good evening, George.'

Then she was turning to himself, the fierce eyes beneath their arched brows sweeping him from head to foot, the carefully painted mouth stretching in a wintry smile.

'My dear Alexander. Quite a stranger.'

Alex took her hand, and kissed the scented cheek. 'Never to you, Gran dear.'

'Hmm.' Selina Perrin made her way to the other sofa, and sat with an effort, accepting the dry sherry that Alex brought her with a word of thanks. 'Now, come and sit with me, and tell me everything you've been doing—apart from what I read about in the papers, of course. There's quite enough of that.'

'Ah,' Alex said lightly. 'You should never believe all the papers say. But I've always thought that if you work hard, you should be allowed to play hard too.'

'I have no objection to that,' she said. 'Just to your occasional choice of playmate. And don't glare at your father,' she added calmly. 'He didn't tell me about the Crosby woman. I already knew.'

Alex bit his lip. 'What a pity you never worked for MI5, darling.'

'There weren't the same openings for women in my day.' She paused. 'Isn't it time, Alexander, that you left other men's wives alone, and found a decent, respectable girl of your own? Settled down?'

He'd expected a sly ambush over dinner, not this frontal attack, and had to make a swift recovery.

'How dull you make it sound, Gran,' he said lightly. 'Besides, I'd be the last man on earth a girl like that would want to marry.'

'Specious nonsense,' Lady Perrin said contemptuously. 'And you know it. You're doing the family no credit, Alexander, and it has to stop. And I refuse to allow the bank to be affected by your rackety behaviour. You're—what? Thirty-three?'

'Thirty-two,' he said, instantly cross with himself for rising to the bait.

'Precisely. You should have sown your wild oats by now.'

He was seething inwardly. 'Perhaps you'd like to suggest a suitable candidate?'

'I could suggest dozens,' his grandmother said calmly. 'But I certainly wouldn't jeopardise their chances by naming them.'

In spite of himself, he found his lips twitching. 'Gran, you're impossible.'

'I'm also serious,' Lady Perrin returned implacably. 'It's my birthday in three months' time. I shall expect you to attend it with your bride.'

Alex was shaken to the roots. From the opposite sofa, he could see his father staring at them both in open incredulity.

He said quietly, 'Darling, that's quite impossible. You must see that. How could I possibly meet someone…persuade her to marry me in that sort of time frame?'

'You are wealthy, clearly attractive to women, and blessed with far more charm than you deserve.' Selina Perrin's tone

was resolute. 'It should be entirely within your capabilities.'
She paused. 'I would not wish to be disappointed.'

The warning was there—implicit—staring him in the face.

He said, with a touch of desperation, 'Grandmother…'

'Besides,' she went on, as if he had not spoken,
'Rosshampton is a family house—a home waiting to be occupied. I must warn you, Alexander, that I should not wish it to
become a bachelor pad. Or, indeed, permit that to happen. Do
I make myself clear?'

Alex stared at her, the colour draining from his face, the
blood drumming in his ears.

He said hoarsely, 'Clear as crystal.' And saw her give a brief,
satisfied smile.

Reaching for her cane, she rose purposefully to her feet.
'Then let us go into dinner. I hope you're both hungry.'

He couldn't speak for his father, Alex thought grimly as he
followed her to the door, but his own appetite had been killed
stone dead.

He'd come prepared for disapproval, and instead been pre-
sented with an ultimatum.

But he wasn't going to let Rosshampton go without a struggle, he told himself. And, although she was infuriating, he did
love his grandmother.

If his inheritance depended on him finding a girl to marry
in the next three months, then a wife he would have.

But a wife on my own terms, he thought as he took his place
at the dining table. Not yours—my dear, clever Gran. And
we'll see, shall we, who has the last laugh?

CHAPTER ONE

'LOUISE—are you up there? What on earth are you doing?'

Louise Trentham, on her knees in the loft, surrounded by open trunks full of elderly clothing, heard her stepmother's querulous tones from the landing below, and grimaced faintly.

'I'm looking for thirties evening dresses,' she called back. 'For the Village Players.'

'Well, come down, please,' Marian Trentham said sharply. 'I can't conduct a conversation peering up into a hole.'

Lou sighed inwardly, but made her way over to the hatch, and swung slim, denim-clad legs onto the loft ladder.

'Is something wrong?' she enquired as she made her way down. 'I made up the rooms as you told me, and did the flowers. And all the food is in the refrigerator, ready for Mrs Gladwin.'

'That's the trouble,' Mrs Trentham said crossly. 'She's just telephoned to say her eldest child is ill again, and she won't be able to cook dinner tonight. And she knows how important this evening is.'

Lou reflected drily that there probably wasn't a soul in the known universe who wasn't aware that Alex Fabian was coming for the weekend. And why.

She said, 'It's hardly her fault. Tim can't help being asthmatic.' She paused. 'Why don't you have dinner at the Royal Oak instead?'

'At a public house?' Mrs Trentham reared back as if her stepdaughter had suggested a visit to a burger joint.

'A very upmarket one,' Lou pointed out. 'With a restaurant in all the food guides. In fact, you'll be lucky to get a table.'

'Because it's intended to be a quiet family meal,' Marian Trentham said tartly.

13

'Offering Alex Fabian a preview of domestic bliss?' Lou's cool face relaxed into a sudden grin. 'From what I hear, he'd prefer the Royal Oak any day of the week.'

Her stepmother's lips thinned. 'Please don't be more irritating than you can help, Louise. On an occasion like this, the right atmosphere is essential.'

'Shouldn't he and Ellie create their own ambience?' Lou enquired mildly. 'Especially when he's sweeping her off her feet into marriage?'

'Well, I don't intend to stand here arguing about it,' Marian Trentham said with finality. 'I simply came to say that you'll have to stand in for Mrs Gladwin, and do the cooking.'

Lou had seen this coming a mile off, and she had no real objections. But the word 'please' would not have come amiss, she thought wryly.

'Shouldn't Ellie do it?' she suggested straight-faced. 'Convince him that she has all the wifely virtues?'

'He's more likely to run out of the house, screaming,' Marian said, with one of her rare glimmers of humour. 'Ellie could burn boiling water. Not that it matters, of course,' she added, reverting to briskness. 'When she's married, there'll be staff to attend to that kind of thing.'

'Of course there will,' Lou murmured. 'Silly me.'

There's staff here too, she thought. And I seem to be it.

'So that's settled, is it?' said Marian. 'You'll cook tonight's dinner? I thought you might do that mushroom soup you're so good at—and an orange sauce with the ducks.'

'Fine,' Lou said equably. 'And, having done so, am I expected to join this quiet family party?'

Marian hesitated for a micro-second too long. 'But of course. If you'd like to. It's entirely up to you, naturally.'

Lou took pity on her. 'Actually, I think I'll pass. Odd numbers and all that. And anyway, I have to go out. There's a rehearsal at the village hall, and I need to get these costumes settled.'

Marian's eyes took on that slightly glazed look which appeared when village matters were under discussion. Marian was a big-city woman. She liked the idea of a weekend country home—something to mention casually in conversation, and invite people to—rather than the reality of it. And she took a minimal part in local activities.

'Well, just as you please,' she said, adding, 'Lou, dear,' as an afterthought. 'And see if you can find something for Ellie to do, would you?' She attempted a silvery laugh. 'She's getting absurdly nervous, silly girl.'

Left to herself, Lou replaced the loft ladder thoughtfully. She didn't mind being part-time caretaker in the house where she'd been born and keeping it pristine for the occasional descents from London by the rest of her family. But sometimes she felt a flicker of resentment at being taken so much for granted.

But it wouldn't be for much longer, she thought, giving herself a mental shake. Because she too was getting married, and would be moving to the tall Georgian house in the main square which belonged to David Sanders, her future husband, who would be furious if he discovered she was acting as head cook and bottle-washer again.

'They're just using you, darling,' he told her over and over again. 'And you're too sweet to mind.'

Lou had never regarded herself as particularly sweet, but it was nice to hear, she acknowledged contentedly.

She shrugged. 'It's no big deal. And it gives me something to do when you're away.'

David worked for the regional office of a national firm of auctioneers and valuers. A recent promotion had involved him in a lot more travelling, and attendance at a series of courses in London, which had left Lou to her own devices more than she cared for, if she was honest.

Her own day job was working as a paralegal at the leading firm of solicitors in the nearby market town. The plan was that she would go on working until they started a family.

She loved the sound of that. Loved the thought of the future they would have together. It seemed to her that there had never been a time when David had not been a part of her life. They'd played as children, fought and made up again as teenagers, and rediscovered each other when he came back from university. And for the past year they'd been unofficially engaged.

It would have been put on a formal footing with a party for family and friends but for the sudden death of David's father, and his mother's subsequent refusal to cope with anything that approximated to 'happy'.

'She will come to the wedding, won't she?' Lou had asked at one point, with a faint irony that was lost on David.

'Of course,' he'd said, kissing her. 'She just needs time, that's all. Be patient.'

Secretly, Lou found patience difficult with David's mother, whom she suspected to be milking widowhood for all it was worth. For one thing, it provided her with an excuse not to leave the family home, which now technically belonged to her son, and move to the bungalow in Bournemouth that she was to share with her sister. Something which had been planned forever, but which now seemed to have been shifted to the back burner.

But it would have to happen sooner or later, Lou assured herself. Because she was congenitally unfitted to share a roof with Mrs Sanders, and David knew it.

So, for the time being, she occupied Virginia Cottage in peace, most of the time, occasionally allowing herself memories of the time when she'd lived there with her mother, enjoying much the same placid existence, with her father coming home at weekends from Trentham Osborne, the independent publishing company which he ran in Bloomsbury.

But following Anne Trentham's shocking and unexpected death after a two-day illness from a strain of viral pneumonia, Lou's whole life had changed. She had been sent away to boarding-school, and her holidays had been spent with Aunt Barbara, her mother's only sister, her big farmer husband and their rowdy, kind, loving family.

But no sooner had she become adapted to this new set of circumstances than they changed too. Her father, his eyes sliding away in embarrassment, had told her that he was getting married again, and she would have a stepmother and sister.

Ellie would be going to the same school, and the rest of the time would be divided between the flat in London and Virginia Cottage.

In retrospect, Lou could see that her father had been involved with Marian long before her mother's death, and that Ellie might well be her half-sister, but by the time she was old enough to realise this, it no longer seemed to matter that much. Marian could be kind enough when she remembered. And Ellie—well, Ellie truly deserved David's epithet 'sweet'.

She was blonde like her mother, but lacked Marian's statuesque build. She was small, blue-eyed and shy, with a pretty, heart-shaped face, in total contrast to Lou, who was taller, and thin rather than slender, with a cloud of unruly dark hair. Lou had pale, creamy skin, and long-lashed grey eyes that were undoubtedly the best feature in a face that she herself dismissed as nondescript. And she had learned, over the years, to appear calm and self-contained.

At school she had soon found herself Ellie's unofficial protector, and she seemed to have carried this role into their adult lives, although, admittedly, she didn't see as much of her stepsister these days, as Ellie lived and worked in London as a copy-editor for Trentham Osborne.

And now, with amazing suddenness, Ellie was going to be married, and someone else would be looking after her. Someone called Alex Fabian.

'I met him at the office,' she'd confided to Louise only a few weeks before. 'Apparently he's a banker, and Daddy and he were doing some kind of business deal.' She frowned. 'I didn't think he'd really noticed me, but he rang the next day and asked me to go to the theatre.'

'Terrific,' Lou said absently, focusing rather on the words "business deal". 'Is Dad looking to re-capitalise?' she enquired.

Ellie shrugged. 'I don't know. But we are bringing out the new art and architecture list, and they say times are hard for independents in publishing.'

'They always were,' said Lou.

Gradually, through Ellie's artless disclosures, she began to build up a picture of this Alex Fabian. He was, it seemed, absolutely gorgeous. There wasn't a club where he wasn't a member, or a restaurant where he couldn't get a table. He was usually seen out with models, actresses and rich girls-about-town. Everywhere they went, he was recognised.

Why, only the other evening they'd gone to the launch of a new brasserie, and this stunning woman, tall with red hair and a fantastic figure, had come up to their table. Alex hadn't seemed very pleased to see her, but he'd called her 'Cindy' and she'd asked him if this was the sacrificial lamb.

Ellie had mentioned this later, and Alex had said that Cindy had a sense of humour all her own, and Ellie wasn't to worry about it. But wasn't it strange?

'Weird,' Lou had agreed with total sincerity.

As she went downstairs she found herself wondering yet again what someone like Alex Fabian was doing with Ellie, who was gentle to the point of naïveté, and certainly no party animal. In fact, she still lived at her parents' flat under Marian's watchful eye.

And what was Ellie's slant on all this? She talked about fabulous meals she'd eaten, and celebrities she'd met. She mentioned the opera, and the ballet, and private viewings at art galleries.

But she said nothing about Alex Fabian himself, the man who was providing all these earthly delights. And demanding—what, in return? Just, it seemed, the pleasure of Ellie's company.

Maybe he'd recognised her intrinsic innocence, and decided to respect it, although that kind of consideration seemed unlikely from someone who clearly lived his life on the fast track.

So, perhaps it was just the attraction of opposites. Whatever, he was coming down this weekend to become formally engaged to Ellie, having apparently first sought the permission of her mother and stepfather.

Very dear and old-fashioned of him, Lou thought, wrinkling her nose in a faint unease she was unable to explain.

And it had resulted in a string of frenetic instructions from Marian, who wanted Virginia Cottage at its quaint and sparkling best, to provide the perfect setting for such a momentous event.

Lou found Ellie in the drawing room, curled up in the corner of a sofa. She didn't fit her mother's description of 'silly' at all. Instead she looked remarkably serious—rather like a small creature caught in the headlights of an oncoming car.

'Hey there,' Lou said gently. 'Come and peel some potatoes for this man of yours. I thought I'd do rosti with the duck.'

'OK. Fine.' Ellie summoned a wan smile as she followed her to the kitchen. She sat at the table, staring without enthusiasm at the bowl of vegetables awaiting her attention.

'Isn't this a little early for bridal nerves?' Lou enquired, surveying her with concern as she handed over an apron and a paring knife, then began swiftly and deftly to prepare the mushrooms for the soup. 'You aren't even engaged yet.'

'No, but I will be in a few hours' time.'

'But only if that's what you want,' Lou countered, frowning. 'So—is it?'

'Of course.' Ellie tilted a charming chin. 'How could it not be?'

'You tell me,' Lou said wryly. 'You look like someone under sentence of death.'

'Don't be absurd,' Ellie said shortly. 'Alex is an incredible man, and I'm going to have an amazing life with him. No one in her right mind is going to turn that away.'

Lou reached for another mushroom. That, she thought, didn't sound like Ellie at all. More as if she was repeating something she'd been told. Something that had been impressed upon her.

I detect Marian's fine white hand in this, she told herself grimly.

She said quietly, 'Ellie—you do love him, don't you?'

'Naturally.' Ellie hacked the skin from an inoffensive potato. 'It's all happened a little fast—that's all.'

'Then tell him you need more time. If he cares for you, he'll understand.'

Ellie shook her head. She said, 'Time is something I—don't have.'

'Oh, God.' Lou came to an apprehensive halt in her preparations. 'Ellie—you're not pregnant, are you?'

Ellie stared at her in astonishment. 'Of course not. How could I possibly be?'

Lou shrugged uncomfortably. 'People in love are usually—lovers too,' she suggested. 'And accidents happen.'

Her stepsister flushed. 'Well, not in our case. Because we—don't...'

'Oh,' Lou said, adding mendaciously, 'I see.'

Although she didn't know why she should be so surprised, she thought, turning back to the mushrooms. After all, sex before marriage wasn't obligatory. And in a sharp-eyed village, where any kind of privacy was at a premium, and your beloved still resided with a mother who tracked his every move, it was virtually impossible, as she knew to her cost.

But, as David had said ruefully, there was no real hurry when they had the rest of their lives together. And what could she do but reluctantly agree?

However, Alex Fabian didn't live his life under the spotlight of parental disapproval, she thought. On the contrary. So, why this uncharacteristic restraint?

She said, 'Then what's the matter? Because there's clearly something.'

Ellie was silent for a moment. She said, 'He—he scares me a little. To be honest, he always has.'

'Then why on earth did you go out with him?' Lou demanded, bewildered.

Ellie shrugged. 'Oh, I wasn't very happy at the time,' she said evasively. 'I thought it might—take my mind off things.'

'And did it?'

Ellie's laugh sounded a little forced. 'Well, of course. Alex demands—total concentration at all times. And now we're going to be married,' she added brightly. 'So everything's worked out for the best.'

'In this best of all possible worlds,' Lou murmured with

irony. 'And maybe you should leave the potatoes to me, love. There'll be none left at the rate you're going.'

'Oh, Lou, I'm sorry.' Ellie looked with contrition at the results of her labours.

'Don't worry about it.' Lou rinsed her hands. 'The future Mrs Fabian will never have to bother with such mundane tasks, anyway. So go and make yourself look gorgeous for him.'

'Yes,' Ellie said slowly. 'I suppose so.' She looked up at the clock, her expression blank. 'He'll be here soon. Time's running out.' And she wandered off, leaving Lou staring after her, perplexed, and frankly worried.

Ellie, she thought, bore no resemblance to a girl about to say 'yes' to the man she adored.

She wondered if she ought to talk to Marian about it, then dismissed the idea, knowing that it would be seen as interference rather than intervention.

And Ellie wasn't a child any more. She had to work out her own salvation. And whether that would include Alex Fabian was entirely her own decision.

Left to herself, she worked steadily, and competently. Soon the ducklings were waiting on their rack, the vegetables prepared, the soup simmering, and a bowl of Chantilly cream whisked up to accompany the dessert of fresh local strawberries.

As David's wife, she might always have to do her own cooking, she thought with faint amusement, but she didn't have one iota of envy for Ellie's carefree future. David was her rock, and she'd never entertained the slightest doubt about him.

Dinner was to be served at eight o' clock, so she now had a breathing space to go back into the loft and choose the dresses to take down to the village hall later.

It was a fascinating task. Like most lofts, it was crammed with remnants of the past, including a lot of old photograph albums, and Lou was constantly being sidetracked.

'Oh, hell,' she muttered as she glanced at her watch. 'It's time those ducklings were in the oven. I'd better get cracking.'

She picked up the armful of dresses she'd chosen. They were

too bulky to manage safely on the ladder, she decided. Much better for them to go first.

She dropped them through the hatch, and was about to follow, when a startled cry reached her from below.

Glancing down in sudden apprehension, Lou saw the dresses seemed to have taken on a life of their own. Were, in fact, on the move. And under their concealing folds a muffled male voice was swearing angrily.

'Oh, God.' Lou scrambled down the ladder at neck-breaking speed. She grabbed a handful of satin, and hauled it away. 'I—I'm so sorry. I didn't realise anyone would be there.'

Her victim shook himself free, his impatient glance flicking over her. 'Really?' he drawled. 'I thought it might be some bizarre rite of passage.'

And Lou realised, horrified, she was taking her first look at Alex Fabian. In the flesh, she thought, swallowing.

He was tall and lean, with broad shoulders and endless legs. His hair, dishevelled from its close encounter with several pounds of fabric, was thick and tawny, and curled slightly. Lou remembered Ellie once saying that his nickname in the City was the Lion King, and could understand why.

He was not conventionally handsome, but he was arrestingly, dynamically attractive, with high cheekbones, glinting green eyes under heavy lids, and a firmly sculpted, almost insolent mouth.

And he was frighteningly, effortlessly sexy. A man who did not have to try, she thought instantly, and wondered how she could possibly know.

A shiver traced its way down her spine. And she thought, 'Poor Ellie.'

Alex Fabian was looking at her too. Lou recognised with shock that she had been stripped, assessed and dismissed in one devastating and totally male glance. A conditioned reflex, she told herself angrily. That's all it was. See a woman—imagine her naked. He probably can't help himself.

But all the same she resented it, even as she realised he was speaking to her again.

He said softly, 'And who are you?'

Lou gave him a bland smile. 'The cook.'

'Indeed?' His brows lifted. He stirred the mass of shimmering cloth at his feet with the toe of a polished shoe. 'Is it part of the job to dress for dinner?'

'No,' she said. 'These are for the local drama group. They're doing a revue—*An Evening with Noël Coward.*'

'Dear God,' said Alex Fabian, and his lips twitched into an appreciative grin. 'A little ambitious, wouldn't you say?'

Lou had thought exactly the same when the idea was first mooted, but she stonily refused to share his amusement. Particularly when his smile had sent his attraction quotient soaring into some sexual stratosphere.

'Don't worry,' she said crisply. 'You won't be expected to buy a ticket.'

'Ah,' he said. 'I've just realised. You're Louise, Ellie's step-sister. How do you do? I'm Alex Fabian.'

Lou dived to pick up the dresses, pretending not to have seen his outstretched hand. It occurred to her that she did not want to touch him. That even a polite handshake might carry some inherent risk, like making contact with a force field. And that she could not afford to find out.

'Yes,' she said. 'I'd gathered who you were.' She hoisted the pile of silks and satins into her arms, using them as a barrier. 'Now you must excuse me. Duty calls.'

'You mean you really are doing the cooking?'

'Well, don't sound so surprised. Someone has to.' She gave him a swift, taut smile. 'Reliable staff is hard to come by round here. But I promise not to poison you.'

'I'm completely reassured.' He paused. 'Before I was booby-trapped,' he said, 'I was looking for the guest bathroom.'

'Second door on the left.' She edged round him.

'One moment,' he said, and a sudden tremor went through her as she felt his hand brush her hair.

She practically jumped backwards, nearly flattening herself against the wall. She said breathlessly, 'Just—what do you think you're doing?'

'Relax,' he advised, a sudden glint in those amazing eyes. 'You had a cobweb in your hair. See?' He showed her its remains on his fingertips. 'Some poor spider is now homeless.'

'A banker with a caring side,' she said. 'I'm impressed.'

'Now, why do I find that so hard to believe?' Alex Fabian said musingly. 'But I won't detain you now for any further discussion. You have your pots and pans to get back to. So, as Noël Coward himself would have put it, Miss Louise Trentham, I'll see you again.'

No, she thought with relief. No, you won't.

Tonight she would be at the village hall, and tomorrow she would persuade David to take her out for the whole day. And on Sunday she'd invent a headache, and stay in her room until they'd all gone back to London.

She muttered something unintelligible into the pile of dresses, and headed off to her room.

Once safely inside, she leaned back against the door panels, and whispered, 'Phew.'

So that was Alex Fabian, she thought weakly. Hell's bells, he should carry a government health warning. No wonder Ellie was becoming flaky at the prospect of marriage with him.

Nor was he a picture of the eager suitor. He was a cool operator. She had seen no kindness in that smiling mouth, no warmth to soften the sensual speculation in the green eyes. For Alex Fabian, women were no more than a commodity to be enjoyed. And what happened when a particular commodity began to pall?

Did Ellie really have the emotional and mental stamina to cope with someone like him? Or was she too glamoured—too beguiled by his looks, charisma and money to care?

She should turn him down, she told herself vehemently. Instantly, and without a second thought. It was a question of survival—pure and simple.

A description which could never be applied to the bride-groom-to-be, she added, her mouth twisting wryly.

She left the dresses on her bed. As she turned away she caught sight of herself in the mirror, and realised there was a smudge of dust on her cheek that Alex Fabian had not seen fit to mention.

Thank God he didn't try to remove it as well, she thought caustically as she went down to the kitchen, or I'd probably be a gibbering wreck by now.

She was concocting the orange sauce for the ducklings when Marian came in.

'Is everything under control?' she demanded, glancing sharply around her.

'In here, it is.' Lou added a dash of Cointreau. 'I can't speak for the rest of the house.'

Marian stared at her. She was elegant in amethyst jersey, with pearls at her throat and in her ears, and her blonde hair was drawn back into an elaborate chignon. 'What is that supposed to mean?'

'I met Ellie's intended,' Lou returned. She paused. 'Are you really going to let her marry him?'

Marian's brows lifted haughtily. 'I think that is a decision that we can safely leave to them.'

'I don't agree.' Lou met her gaze calmly and directly. 'I think it's like handing a lamb over to a tiger.'

'What a dramatic turn of phrase,' her stepmother said mockingly. 'Perhaps you should be writing melodramas for your little village group.'

'Better melodrama than tragedy,' Lou said curtly. 'Marian, she's not in his league. You must see that.'

'I see that she's marrying a very successful man, who will soon be chairman of Perrins Bank,' Marian retorted.

'So you're not pretending she loves him.'

Marian laughed. 'Oh, I think she'll find it very easy to love him—in the ways that matter to a man. After all, she'll have an expert teacher.' She paused. 'Are you quite sure, Lou, dear, that you're not just a tiny bit jealous?

'No,' Lou said steadily. 'Because I have a man that I can love in all the ways there are. Not just those that happen in the bedroom.'

'You're really a little prude, aren't you?' Marian drawled. 'I'm sure you and David will suit each other admirably.' She glanced at her diamond watch. 'Are you leaving yourself enough time to change?'

'I'm going to a village-hall rehearsal, not Glyndebourne.' Lou tasted her sauce, and nodded with satisfaction.

'But you can't serve the dinner in jeans and an old sweater.'

'I've no intention of serving it at all,' Lou retorted curtly. 'I said I'd cook, and that's it. You and Ellie can manage the rest between you—unless, of course, you want Alex Fabian to end up with a lap full of mushroom soup,' she added menacingly. 'No? I thought not. And I presume you know how to load the dishwasher as well,' she called after her stepmother as Marian flounced out.

A minor victory, she thought, but what did that matter when the war was already lost?

Up in her room, she went across to the window to close the curtains against the gathering twilight, and paused, alerted by a movement in the shrubbery below her. To her surprise, she saw it was Ellie, pacing up and down, and talking on her cell-phone.

What on earth is she doing out there? Lou asked herself in bewilderment. 'I'd have thought Marian would have had her chained to Alex Fabian's wrist by now.'

She was about to rap on the window—attract Ellie's attention—then held back. Even in the poor light, she could see that her stepsister looked strained. Every gesture, every restless movement betrayed her agitation.

Maybe she's decided she can't go through with it, she thought. But who is she talking to? The Samaritans?

She went back to the bed and began shaking out the dresses, folding them with care and placing them in large carriers.

On her way out to the car she would have a word with Ellie, she decided. Tell her that she, at least, was on her side.

But when she got outside, there was no one about. As she went past the dining-room window she glanced in, and saw Ellie sitting next to Alex Fabian at the candlelit table, talking and laughing as if she didn't have a care in the world.

The Samaritans must do a wonderful job, Lou thought with a resigned sigh, and went to her rehearsal.

The carrier bags were seized on joyfully by the female cast members and taken off to the women's dressing room. Lou found a chair and sat down to watch while she waited for David to arrive. He didn't act in any of the village productions but he helped with scenery and lighting, and he was coming to discuss the design of the set with Ray, the producer.

Lou hadn't attended any rehearsals for a couple of weeks, and she was amazed to find what progress they'd made. Even Ray who was also playing Noël Coward, was far better than she'd expected.

Then the girls came back in the evening dresses she'd brought, and paraded them on stage for Ray to make a final choice, and it was only when she was re-packing the rejected ones that she realised how late it was getting.

'Where on earth is David?' she asked Ray.

For a moment he looked blank, then, 'Oh, he phoned earlier, just before you got here, love. Said something had cropped up, and he couldn't make it.'

Lou frowned. 'He didn't call me.'

'He probably took it for granted I'd tell you,' Ray said peaceably. 'Which I now have.'

'He didn't say what the problem was?'

'No,' Ray admitted. 'But I expect his mother's thrown another wobbly. He'd hardly want that generally known.' He paused. 'You haven't got any tailcoats or top hats in that loft of yours, by any chance?'

She forced a smile. 'I didn't notice any, but I'll have a good look tomorrow.'

She took the long route back to Virginia Cottage, going through the square, but David's house was all in darkness, so she drove on without stopping.

Perhaps Ray had been quite right about his mother, she thought. And once David had managed to get her calm again, he'd decided to have an early night. Well, she couldn't blame him for that, and nor would she.

But all the same, it was disappointing not to have seen him, and she wished very much that he'd rung her to explain. No doubt he'd ring in the morning, and they'd arrange to spend the day together then.

To her surprise, all the lights were out at Virginia Cottage too. She'd expected to find a party going on, but perhaps there was nothing to celebrate after all.

She parked at the rear, beside the low, sleek sports car that looked so alien in the cobbled yard, and went in through the back door. Her immediate intention was to make herself a hot drink, but that was before she saw the state the kitchen was in.

Clearly Marian had decided the dishwasher was unknown territory after all, she thought grimly, because all the plates, cutlery, dishes and pans used for the meal were piled haphazardly on every surface.

She was half tempted to leave them there, except for the knowledge that they would still be waiting for her in the morning, and she hated that.

David is quite right, she thought, smouldering. They do use me. But this is the last time.

She filled the kettle and set it to boil, then began the dreary task of rinsing the crockery, and putting it in the dishwasher.

The running water disguised the sound of the kitchen door opening behind her, and she only realised she was no longer alone when Alex Fabian said, 'Good evening, Cinderella. Did the ball end early?'

He was standing just behind her. Close enough, she thought, to touch.

Her whole body clenched in sudden, uncontrollable panic, and the dish she was holding slipped from her hands, and smashed into fragments on the quarry-tiled floor between them.

Then there was silence.

CHAPTER TWO

A SILENCE that Alex Fabian was the first to break.

He said, 'I seem to have startled you. I'm sorry. I hope the breakage won't be stopped out of your wages,' he added smoothly.

Lou glared at him. He'd discarded the jacket and tie he'd been wearing at dinner, and his white shirt was half-unbuttoned, revealing more than she wished to see of a brown, muscular chest. His cuffs were undone and turned casually back over equally tanned forearms.

She said, 'What the hell do you think you're doing—creeping around at this time of night?'

'This time of night?' he echoed derisively. 'Lady, in London the evening would just be beginning.'

'Well, we don't go in much for big-city nightlife round here,' Lou said curtly.

'I gathered that,' he said drily. 'On the stroke of midnight, everyone turns back into pumpkins.'

'You should have made it clear you wanted to be entertained.' Lou went over to the broom cupboard in the corner, and extracted a dustpan and brush. 'I'm sure my family would have turned cartwheels for you.'

Alex Fabian whistled softly. 'I get the distinct impression, Miss Trentham, that you don't like me very much.'

'Fortunately, I don't have to.' She began to sweep up the broken pieces. 'We inhabit totally different worlds, Mr Fabian.'

'Worlds which seem to have collided,' he said. 'I'm about to become part of the family. Aren't you going to congratulate me?'

She emptied the dustpan into the rubbish bin with a clatter. 'On having got what you want? I imagine that's the norm for you. Besides, with all you have to offer, how could Ellie possibly resist?'

'I admit I thought she'd respond better to the carrot than the stick.' He seemed amused, rather than offended. 'I'm glad you agree.'

'Well, I'm not glad about any of it. And where is Ellie, anyway?'

'She opted for an early night, and the others followed,' he said. His mouth twisted. 'I think the excitement was all too much for her.'

Lou went on loading the dishwasher. She said in a low voice, 'I think you're too much for her. Don't you know that she's frightened of you?'

'No,' Alex Fabian said quietly, after a pause. 'I didn't realise that. But she truly has nothing to be scared of. Maybe I didn't make that as clear as I should have done.'

'Ellie's a beautiful girl, but she's also fragile. She needs kindness, Mr Fabian. I'm not sure you have much of that to spare.'

'Then maybe that's a trait we share, Miss Trentham.' His voice was suddenly harsh. 'You're very ready to condemn on very little evidence. I promise you on my word of honour that Ellie has nothing to fear from me. That I will look after her as my wife, and treat her well. Does that satisfy you?'

'Perhaps it's her that you should reassure.'

His mouth tightened. 'I would have done, if I'd had the chance to be alone with her before she scuttled off to bed. As a matter of fact, I tapped on her door just now and spoke to her in case she was still awake, but there was no answer.'

'She probably thought you wanted more than conversation.' The words were out before she could stop them.

'Oh, God,' Lou muttered under her breath. 'I've done it now.' And she bent swiftly to put the detergent tablet in the machine to disguise the fact that she was blushing.

He said quite mildly, 'Now, why should she think any such thing? As you're so much in her confidence, you must know I've made no demands of that kind.'

'Yes, but you're engaged now. Officially. That—changes things.' Lou, having dug the hole and fallen into it, was now sinking rapidly. She shut the machine door, and switched on the programme. Anything not to have to look at him. Or hear him. Or even share the same universe with him, she thought detachedly.

'Does it indeed?' he said, and she could hear the unholy amusement quivering in his voice. 'Well, I've never been engaged before, so I bow to your superior wisdom. Should I rush upstairs and ravish her now, do you think, or can it wait until tomorrow night?

'You see, I'd actually planned to make myself some coffee, and do a couple of hours' work on my laptop, but I'm prepared to make the sacrifice, if necessary,' he added piously.

'This is all a big joke to you, isn't it?' Lou swung round and faced him stormily.

'Think what you want.' He shrugged. 'If I told you the truth, you wouldn't believe me. And the kettle's boiling. Shall I make us both some coffee?'

'I'm having herb tea.' If it was an olive branch, Lou didn't want it. 'I don't drink coffee at this hour. It keeps me awake.'

'How naughty of it,' Alex Fabian said gravely. 'Of course, there are a lot of far more pleasurable activities that have exactly the same effect, but perhaps you haven't tried those.'

Helplessly, Lou felt her face warming again. She went over to the cupboard, produced two beakers, set them on the worktop, and pushed the coffee jar towards him without a word.

'Before you flounce out of the room, slamming the door behind you,' Alex Fabian said pleasantly, spooning granules into his beaker and adding boiling water, 'I should tell you that was a magnificent dinner you gave us tonight.'

'Thank you.' The beguiling aroma of coffee seemed to fill the kitchen. Biting her lip, Lou dropped a camomile tea bag into her beaker, and let it infuse.

'Have you ever thought of cooking professionally?' he went on. 'Private lunch and dinner parties in people's homes? I should think you'd make a fortune.'

'On the contrary,' Lou said. 'In future, I intend to cook only for my husband.'

He gave her bare left hand a fleeting glance. 'Does this fortunate guy exist, or is he simply an erotic fantasy in your caffeine-free dreams?'

'Of course he's real. I—I thought you knew I was engaged.' Her flush deepened.

'Ah,' he said. 'Our brief debate on sexual etiquette. I thought you knew that was a wind-up.'

'And Ellie didn't tell you?'

'Ellie,' he said, 'has told me very little. But I haven't exactly been forthcoming myself, so I can hardly complain.' He paused. 'So, who is he?'

'Someone I've known forever. He lives in the village, and works for Galbraiths in their regional office.'

'Does he have a name?'

'He's called David Sanders.' Her tone was short. 'Why do you ask?'

'So that when I come to your wedding I'll know what to call the groom,' Alex Fabian said calmly. 'I presume, as Ellie's husband, I'll receive an invitation.'

Ellie's husband, she thought. *Ellie's husband?* If she lived to be a thousand, she could never see him in any such role.

She said slowly, 'I suppose so.' She fished out the tea bag and disposed of it. 'Do you want milk in your coffee?'

'I take it black,' he said. 'It helps me stay awake.'

'Of course,' she said. 'You have work to do. Please don't let me keep you.'

'I am working,' he said, and smiled at her with faint mockery. 'Building bridges, I hope, with my future sister-in-law.' He leaned against the kitchen table and took a meditative sip of coffee. 'Tell me, how is it you don't work for Trentham Osborne as Ellie does?'

'Because publishing never appealed to me, and London certainly didn't. I was always happiest here, so I moved back permanently and got a job with a local law firm.'

'You're a solicitor?'

She bit her lip. 'No, a paralegal. I went to the same school as Ellie, and they weren't geared up for university grades, just...' She hesitated.

'Just grooming the girls to make suitable marriages?' he prompted softly.

'Actually—yes,' Lou acknowledged ruefully. She shook her head. 'You wouldn't believe that it could still go on.'

'No?' He drank some more coffee, watching her over the rim of the beaker. 'Yet it seems to have worked for you.'

'David isn't "suitable" in that sense,' she said. As her stepmother never failed to make clear, she thought wryly. 'Just— the right man for me.'

'How fortunate you are,' he said softly. 'To be so certain so early in your life.'

'Yes,' she said, 'I think I am.'

She finished her tea, and rinsed her beaker briskly under the tap. She gave him a bright, meaningless smile. 'Well—good-night. Will you switch off the lights as you go up?'

At the door, she paused. She said haltingly, 'And I'm sorry for the way I spoke earlier. I—I hope that you and Ellie will be very happy together.'

The green eyes met hers, cool and enigmatic.

'I feel sure,' he said, 'that her old school would be proud of her. Goodnight—sister-in-law.'

She was suddenly aware that her heart was thudding quickly—unpredictably. She smiled uncertainly, and went swiftly upstairs to her room. She closed the door behind her and drew a deep breath.

For a moment there, she'd allowed her guard to drop. And had been made aware, in a few devastating seconds, how disturbing a man Alex Fabian could be.

Bad move on her part, she thought. And lesson duly learned. From now on she would take more care. And keeping out of his way was just the first step.

Lou was tired when she climbed into bed, but sleep proved elusive just the same. She found her mind was churning, going over her encounter with Alex in the kitchen, and trying to analyse what had been said, and what else had been implied.

Oh, this is ridiculous, she adjured herself at last. Forget about the wretched guy, and concentrate on tomorrow.

She supposed, glumly, that if Mrs Gladwin failed to arrive again she would be expected to cook the breakfast, and she would do so, but after that they could forage for themselves, because she was going to the coast with David.

They would have a seafood lunch in a pub, then walk along the beach, and talk seriously about fixing a date for the wedding. It had hardly been mentioned in recent weeks.

Three months ahead, she thought contentedly, would surely give Mrs Sanders plenty of time to move to her sister's place.

When eventually she slept, it was to dream that her wedding day had come, and she was walking up the aisle of the village church on her father's arm to her bridegroom, waiting at the altar.

But as she got nearer he turned his head, and she saw, instead of David's ruggedly familiar and beloved face, a mask, blank and featureless. And, crying out with fear and grief, she fled, alone, back the way she had come.

The dream was still vivid in her mind when she woke. Nasty, she thought, shivering, then threw back the bedclothes. Nothing, especially a nightmare, would be allowed to cloud this lovely day.

She showered, and dressed casually in a knee-length denim skirt and a white short-sleeved top, then brushed her hair into a silky cloud on her shoulders.

Because she would soon be seeing David, she accentuated her eyes with grey shadow and mascara, and coloured her mouth with her favourite dusky rose lipstick before she went downstairs.

When she got to the kitchen she found to her relief that young Tim had recovered from his asthma attack, and Mrs Gladwin was there ahead of her, already assembling the ingredients for the kedgeree and cutting the rind off the bacon rashers.

'I took Mr and Mrs Trentham's tea up to them,' Mrs Gladwin reported. 'But I had to leave Miss Ellie's tray outside her door, as I couldn't make her hear me. And I didn't know what to do about her visitor.'

'I think he'd prefer coffee.' Lou found the small cafetière and filled it. But she had no intention of taking Alex Fabian coffee in bed, she thought, her mouth tightening. That was Ellie's task, and she could wake up and do it.

While she was waiting for the coffee to brew, she popped out into the yard and called David on her mobile, only to discover that his was switched off.

She pulled a face as she returned indoors. If she used the ordinary phone his mother was bound to answer, and be plaintive at the prospect of her boy spending time with anyone else.

But maybe David would call her instead before that happened.

When she went upstairs, she found Ellie's tray still untouched outside her door.

Puzzled, she set the coffee down beside it and knocked. 'Ellie—Ellie, wake up. Your tea's getting cold.'

There was no answer, and, after a moment's hesitation, she opened the door, and looked in.

But there was no blonde head lifting sleepily from the pillow. The bed was empty, and the room unoccupied.

And no prizes for guessing where Ellie was, Lou thought, feeling oddly embarrassed. That neatly made bed was a total giveaway. She must have decided to celebrate her engagement in the arms of her fiancé after all.

'Everyone's still asleep,' she told Mrs Gladwin as she carried all the things back to the kitchen. 'I'm going into the village to get the papers.'

She followed the previous night's detour on the way back. The curtains were still firmly closed on the first floor of David's house, but his car was missing from its usual parking spot outside.

He must have gone to the cottage to find me, Lou thought, her heart lifting. 'We can have breakfast together.'

Yet there was no sign of his blue Peugeot at Virginia Cottage either. Instead, there was Alex Fabian, walking alone in the garden. He was the last person she'd expected to see so early, under the circumstances. And the last person she wanted to see, she amended quickly.

She hesitated, feeling strangely awkward, wondering if there was some way to evade him, but he had already seen her, so she had to reluctantly stand her ground.

'Good morning,' he said as he came up to her. 'Did you sleep well?'

'Yes—thank you.' She stared down at the gravel. 'And—you?'

'Not particularly,' he said. 'The coffee did its work too well.'

She gave a quick, forced smile. 'I'm sure Ellie wouldn't agree.'

'Oh,' he said. 'And how does it concern her?'

'I took her some morning tea,' she said. 'And her bed hadn't been slept in. I—I drew the obvious conclusion.'

His hand closed on her arm. 'Look at me,' he commanded harshly. 'What the hell are you talking about?'

She stared up at him, bewildered. 'Ellie wasn't in her room this morning. I—I thought she was with you.'

'I haven't seen your sister,' he said, 'since nine-thirty yesterday evening, when she decided to have that extremely early night. And the last place she would ever be likely to spend the night is in my bed.'

He set off towards the house, taking Lou with him, whether or not she wished to go.

She tried to hang back. 'I'm sure there's a perfectly logical explanation.' She tried to think of one. 'Perhaps she got up early, and went for a walk.'

'Walking,' he said, 'is not one of her pastimes. Your sister believes in taxis, when chauffeur-driven cars aren't available. I think you know that.'

'Maybe there's been some emergency at the office, and she's had to go back to London.' Lou clutched at a passing straw.

'If so, I think they'd probably have sent for your father,' he said. 'And he's still here.'

In the hall, Marian greeted Alex, all smiles. 'Breakfast is ready, if you'd like to come into the dining room.'

He said, 'Have you seen Ellie this morning, Mrs Trentham? Because Louise says her bed has not been slept in.'

Marian's hand went to her throat. 'Oh, what nonsense. I expect she was just too happy and excited to sleep.'

'All the same, with your permission, I'd like to look in her room.'

Lou tried to detach herself from his grasp. 'I'd rather not...'

'I'm afraid you must,' he said. 'You can tell me if anything's missing.'

My God, Lou thought as she followed him unwillingly upstairs. She's done it. She's decided she can't go through with the engagement, and she's run away. And, if that's so, I should be delighted for her. So why do I feel so scared suddenly?

'Well?' Alex demanded as they stood in the middle of Ellie's bedroom, looking round them.

Lou swallowed. 'The case she brought down with her has gone.' She opened the wardrobe, and looked in the drawers. 'And she seems to have taken underwear and some clothes.'

'And left these.' His voice was suddenly grim.

Lou turned to see him holding two envelopes. 'Where did you find them?'

'Propped against the lamp on the night table,' he said. 'One for each of us.' He paused. 'Are you sure you want to open yours?'

'Of course,' Lou said indignantly. 'I'm worried sick about her. I need to make sure she's all right.'

'I think you underestimate her sense of self-preservation,' Alex Fabian said drily as he handed her the envelope.

Her name was a mere scrawl on its surface. Inside was a single sheet of paper. She could barely decipher the writing. 'Lou, darling,' she eventually translated, 'I'm so terribly sorry. Please try to understand and forgive me.'

'What does it say?' Alex's level voice reached her.

She turned and looked at him. He was holding his own letter, two pages of it, between thumb and forefinger as if he found it distasteful.

She said, 'She wants me to forgive her—but for what? For running away?'

'Not just for that, I'm afraid.' He paused. 'You see, she didn't go alone.'

She saw something in his eyes that she had never expected to find there. Compassion. And it frightened her more than any coldness—any anger.

She tried to say 'What do you mean?' But, although her lips moved, the words would not emerge.

She heard a sound from the doorway, and looked round swiftly, praying it would be Ellie standing there. Ellie, saying it had all been a silly mistake, and here she was, safe and sound.

Only it was her father, his face like thunder.

'Louise—Mrs Sanders has telephoned. Will you come and speak to her, please? She's hysterical—out of control. I can't make out what she's saying. She keeps repeating "David and Ellie" over and over again. I think she must have gone mad.'

'It would be convenient to think so.' Alex Fabian stepped forward to station himself between Lou and her father. Shielding her white face, trembling mouth and wide, bewildered eyes.

'But I'm afraid her hysterics are justified. My erstwhile fiancée has run away with her son, and they're going to be married. She's left me a letter, confessing everything.'

'I don't believe a word of it,' the older man said harshly. 'It must be some sick joke. Good God, man, it was only last night she became engaged to you.'

'Apparently that was the final straw,' Alex told him calmly. 'She and David Sanders had been in love for some time, but they'd tried to behave nobly for Louise's sake—or some such maudlin nonsense. She went out with me to try and forget him, but when she realised marriage was on the agenda she decided she couldn't go through with it after all, and appealed to Sanders to rescue her.

'And—they eloped last night.'

Louise felt totally numb. Presently, she knew, there would be pain. But now there were images passing through her mind like some nightmare slide show. Ellie's frantic phone call. Click. The dark house. Click. The empty space where David's car should have been. Click. Until she wanted to scream.

'Well, they won't get away with it.' Mr Trentham's voice shook. 'I'll have them found. Make her come back.'

'I hope you won't do anything of the kind,' Alex Fabian said coldly. 'She's not a young child. She's a woman, and quite capable of making her own choices. Something we overlooked in our negotiations.'

'Ellie?' Marian Trentham had joined them now, her face ashen, her eyes blazing. 'My beautiful girl with that—that buffoon? It can't be true.'

Lou made a small sound in her throat, and Alex glanced at her sharply. He said, 'Mrs Trentham, I think you've forgotten that Louise was engaged to David Sanders.'

'I haven't forgotten a thing,' the older woman said shrilly. 'It's all her fault—encouraging him to hang round here, where he could meet my lovely Ellie. Of course he preferred her. What man wouldn't?'

'No,' Alex said, studying her with cold dislike, 'according to her letter, they met up in London when he was on some course. So Louise can't possibly be blamed. In fact, she's been subjected to the worst kind of betrayal by both of them.'

Betrayal. The word made Louise shiver, but it brought her back to life. And to unpleasant reality.

She heard herself say, 'Mrs Sanders must still be waiting on the phone. I'd better go and talk to her.'

'No.' Alex halted her, his hand on her arm. 'Your father can do that for you. Or your stepmother,' he added curtly. 'There's no reason why you should be exposed to any more recriminations.'

Her father said hoarsely, 'Yes, of course. I'll go now. Though God knows what I can say…'

As he departed, muttering distractedly, Marian Trentham moved forward, her hands outstretched. 'Alex, my dear.' Her voice throbbed. 'What you must be suffering.'

'I don't appreciate being made a fool of,' Alex said tersely. 'And your daughter's defection is going to cause me immeasurable trouble and inconvenience. But please let's drop the pretence that Ellie and I were ever in love with each other.'

For a moment she faltered, then she returned to the attack, forcing a smile.

'You're hurt,' she said. 'As you have every right to be. I do understand. But all is not yet lost. I think we should go downstairs and have some breakfast, and decide what to do next.'

'I know exactly what I'm doing next,' Alex said coldly. 'I'm going back to London, and I'll forgo your kind offer of breakfast. I'd prefer to be on my way as soon as possible.'

'But there are matters outstanding,' she said rapidly, her voice beginning to shake. 'Things we need to discuss.'

'You mean the re-financing plan? But that was dependent on certain conditions being met, so there is really very little to talk about.'

Louise could hear the words, but she could not grasp what they meant. They seemed to float past her. The room, too, suddenly seemed to be swimming.

She said in a stifled voice, 'I—I think I'm going to be sick.'

During the miserable and humiliating minutes that followed, Louise was dimly aware of an arm supporting her as she retched violently into the lavatory bowl, of a hand smoothing back her hair, and wiping her face with a damp flannel.

'You,' she said shakily as she sat up at last, the tiles on the bathroom walls still swooping dizzily around her. 'Oh, God, it's *you.*'

'Well, who else would it be?' Alex Fabian retorted crushingly. 'Your father's still on the phone, being screamed at, and your stepmother's shut herself into her bedroom. You needed help.'

'You're the last person I'd turn to for that.' She got painfully to her feet. 'If you hadn't pressured Ellie to marry you, none of this would have happened.'

'It would have eventually. A different set of circumstances, perhaps, but the same result.' He shrugged. 'They're in love. They were always going to end up together. I was just the catalyst.'

She glared at him. 'Is that supposed to make me feel better?'

'That's up to you. But I'd say it would be a pretty refined kind of hell to find you'd married a man who wanted someone else. Here, drink this.'

Unwillingly Lou accepted the glass of water he held out to her. She'd just caught a horrified glimpse of herself in the bathroom mirror—her ghost-white face streaked with mascara, her lipstick smeared. The pretty, confident picture she'd painted for David totally ruined. Like her life.

Not only did she look like hell, she thought, writhing inwardly, but she'd just thrown up in front of a man she detested.

She said stiltedly, 'I think I'd like to be alone now.'

'Just as you wish.' He paused. 'I'll have some tea brought up to you.'

'Tea?' Her voice rose. 'My heart is broken, and you offer me—bloody clichés.'

'It's also the classic remedy for shock,' he returned, unperturbed. 'And hearts are more resilient than you think. Would you like me to help you to your room?'

'No,' she said. 'And stop behaving like someone out of a medical drama. Because the best thing you could do for me would be to get out of my sight, and my life.'

'I think,' Alex Fabian said quietly, 'that's something that could be open to discussion. But possibly not at this moment.'

'Not ever,' Lou said fiercely. 'So—please go.'

She turned away, and began to run hot water into the basin, and when she glanced around again she was alone. Which was something she would have to get accustomed to, she realised, wretchedness stabbing her as she washed her face.

With the worst ravages removed, she went back to her room

and threw herself across the bed, digging clenched fists into the coverlet.

Love must indeed be blind, she thought, because she'd never had the slightest idea that David might be looking elsewhere. She'd always felt so happy and comfortable with him, and on the surface everything had seemed just the same.

Yet, she supposed, there had been clues for anyone with a suspicious mind. The fact that David no longer talked about the wedding had been one. And he'd been more preoccupied than usual lately, although he'd blamed problems at work for that.

And Ellie hadn't been the same either, dating Alex Fabian with such feverish, determined enjoyment. As if trying to convince herself that they could have a life together.

You fool, she told herself. You complacent, trusting idiot.

She could sense the tears gathering inside her, threatening to fill the ache of emptiness. And pain was prowling, too, waiting to sink its claws into her heart and mind.

The tap at her door sent her bolt upright, looking apprehensively over her shoulder. But it was only Mrs Gladwin bringing the threatened tea. Her face was solemn, but her eyes, understandably, were sparking with curiosity.

'No one wanted any breakfast,' she said. 'So I've had to throw all that lovely food away. It seems a wicked waste.' She paused. 'I've cleared up the kitchen, so if I'm not wanted for anything else…?'

Lou realised wearily that she was asking to be paid. She forced a smile. 'That's fine, Mrs Gladwin, and thank you.' She found her bag, and handed over the cash.

Mrs Gladwin lingered. 'Next weekend, Miss Louise? Will the family be down?'

Lou looked at her blankly. 'I—I really don't know.' Nor did she care, she thought. And how absurd to think that life could just—go on. For anyone to assume that she would go on living in this house—in this village—with all the dead hopes, dead memories. When everyone must know that was quite impossible.

When she knew, beyond all doubt, that she had to get away—and fast. Leave it all behind her, and escape.

She said quietly, 'I'm sure my stepmother will be in touch over the arrangements. Thank you for the tea.'

'The cup that cheers,' said Mrs Gladwin, nodding portentously, and departed.

Louise looked at the tray, with its snowy lace cloth and the pretty flowered crockery. Another act of kindness, she thought, amid the personal desolation that was beginning to tear at her. But, again, from the wrong person. She did not want Alex Fabian's kindness. She could not bear the thought of it.

She went on staring until the outlines of cup, saucer, jug and teapot lost their separate shapes, and became oddly blurred. Until the first scalding, agonised tears began to sear their way down her face, falling faster and faster.

She began to sob, making small, desperate, uncontrollable noises, pressing her hands over her eyes so that the salty drops squeezed through her fingers. She could feel grief burn in her throat, and taste it on her icy lips.

At some moment, still weeping, she stripped off the skirt and top and threw them across the room, shuddering as if they were rank—rancid. Knowing she never wanted to see them again as long as she lived.

She went to the wardrobe, dragged out a pair of black jeans and a round-necked sweater in fine grey wool, and pulled them onto her body.

She found her soft leather travel bag, and began hurriedly to fill it with underwear, more trousers and casual tops, flat shoes.

Escape, she thought, the word echoing like a mantra in her brain. Escape...

But where could she go?

There was Somerset, she thought. She could stay with her aunt and uncle, and find kindness with them. Use their farm as a sanctuary while she tried to decide what she could do with the rest of her life.

On her way downstairs, she paused outside the main bedroom and tapped on the door.

Her father opened it. 'What is it?' He looked at her bag. 'Is it Ellie? Has she come back?'

'No,' she said, wincing. 'That's—not going to happen, Dad. But I'm going away for a while.'

'But she must come back,' he said. He looked past her. 'You don't realise how serious all this is. It was part of the deal with Fabian, and he's walked out on us. We need that injection of capital, or the business could go under. We could lose everything.'

Lou stared at the man in front of her, and wondered when he had first become a stranger.

She said, 'I think you already have lost everything. At least everything that matters.' She paused. 'I'll be in touch—some time.'

She went out of the cottage the back way, feeling fresh tears springing up as she realised how much of her life she was leaving behind. Yet knowing at the same time that she had no other choice.

She'd expected—hoped—maybe even prayed that Alex Fabian would be long gone. But there was to be no respite for her on this merciless day.

Because, as she came out into the yard, he was there, loading his own bag into the boot of his car.

She checked instantly, wondering if she could duck back into the house before he saw her. But it was too late.

He was already straightening, turning to look at her, the green eyes curiously intent.

'So there you are,' he said softly. 'I've been waiting for you.'

CHAPTER THREE

SHE knew, of course, what he was seeing. The drenched eyes, the trembling mouth, and the pale face smudged with tears. She couldn't even hide behind her hair, because her final act before leaving her room had been to drag it back and confine it at the nape of her neck with an elastic band.

Oh, God, she thought desperately. Why did this man of all men have to be around when she was at her most vulnerable?

She lifted her chin. Kept the betraying quiver from her voice. 'I'm sorry if I've detained you, Mr Fabian, although I can't imagine why that should be. We've said everything that needs to be said, and now we can go our separate ways.'

'Not quite,' he said. 'Where are you going?'

'None of your damned business.' She reached into her shoulder bag, found her sunglasses and jammed them on her nose. One small barrier to shelter behind, she thought, searching for her car keys. 'Will you please leave me alone?'

'No,' he said. He walked across, picked up her travel bag and slung it into the boot of his car next to his own case.

'How dare you?' Lou's voice cracked with outrage. 'What the hell do you think you're doing?'

'Taking over,' he returned tersely. 'Someone needs to. Most families are hell at times, but you seem particularly unlucky in yours. Your sister runs off with your man, and your father and his wife are too caught up in the financial ramifications of it all to notice that you're falling apart.'

'Thank you.' She was shaking again, but this time it was with temper. 'But I can manage on my own.'

The green eyes swept her dismissively. 'Well, you certainly can't drive in that state,' he said. 'You'd kill yourself within a mile.'

46

She glared at him. 'Do you think I'd care?'

'Suicide may have its attractions,' he said, meditatively. 'And the news might well put a temporary blight on married bliss for the happy couple, although I wouldn't count on it. But it also tends to drastically reduce all future options. So I think you should consider living. And living well. That's a far better revenge on your ex-fiancé.'

'Do you think that's what I want—revenge?' Lou was gasping.

'Well, I hope you don't want him back,' he said. 'I should be very disappointed in you, if so.'

'And we couldn't possibly have that, could we?' Her voice dripped scorn. 'Why can't you just get out of my life, Mr Fabian?'

'Because fate seems to have thrown us together, Miss Trentham.' He closed the boot, and walked round to open the passenger door. 'Are you going to tell me where you'd like me to take you, or shall I make it up as I go along?'

'Anywhere—as long as it's away from here.' Lou stayed where she was. 'And away from you,' she added stormily. 'Can't you see that you're the last person I want to have around?'

'That's unfortunate,' Alex drawled. 'Because I really seem to be all you've got. And you must have some destination in mind. You can't have been planning to simply drive until you ran out of petrol.'

'No.' She bit her lip. 'I'm going to Somerset—to stay with my aunt and uncle,' she offered unwillingly.

'Well, that's a first step,' he said. 'And afterwards?'

'I don't know,' she admitted. 'I—I can't seem to think that far ahead. But I can't ever come back here. Everyone in the village knew I was going to marry David. Half of them would have been coming to the wedding. I—I just can't face them all.'

'Don't be a fool,' he said. 'Do you seriously imagine anyone would blame you for what's happened?'

'No.' Her voice broke. 'But they'd feel sorry for me. And that would be the worst—the unbearable thing. To be pitied...'

'I agree,' Alex said briskly. 'Which brings us back to my original suggestion that you should take life by the throat and use it to your own best advantage.'

She gave him a mutinous look, swallowing back the tears which threatened again. 'And you, of course, are full of bright ideas about how I can do that.'

'Perhaps,' he said. 'When you're prepared to listen. In the meantime, get in the car, and I'll take you to Somerset.'

She was suddenly too weary to argue any more. Besides, her bag was shut in his boot, and she suspected it might take an undignified scuffle to retrieve it.

She moved reluctantly towards his car, then halted. 'But you were going back to London,' she objected. 'Won't people wonder where you are?'

'You forget,' Alex said sardonically. 'I'm away for the weekend getting engaged. No one's expecting me back until Monday.' He saw her into the passenger seat, then moved round to the driver's side. 'And a little sympathy for me wouldn't go amiss,' he added. 'I'm also an injured party in this, if you remember.'

'Yes,' Lou said. 'I can see you're totally devastated.'

'I'm actually bloody angry,' he said. 'I just hide it well. Fasten your seat belt.'

'Why—is it going to be a bumpy ride?' Lou's voice held an edge as she complied.

His mouth slanted in a faint smile. 'I'd say that was entirely up to you,' he said softly, and started the engine.

There was a produce market in the village each Saturday morning, so their progress was slowed to a snail's pace.

Lou had expected Alex Fabian to become swiftly impatient at the delay. A powerful man in a powerful car could be an explosive combination, but he seemed cool and relaxed, lost in his own thoughts.

A powerful man, she thought, prepared to play a waiting

game, and bit her lip, realising that she found the idea disturbing.

By now, she knew, she was bound to have been noticed. At any moment, someone might tap on the window and ask where David was—and, by implication, why she was driving through the village with a complete stranger.

A question that she would find it quite impossible to answer. Because she still couldn't believe that she was actually doing this. That she was meekly allowing Alex Fabian to take her all the way to Somerset, with the awful prospect of being cooped up in this car with him for at least two hours.

And he'd made it seem as if it was her only choice, she thought, savaging her lip again.

She sat staring rigidly ahead of her, her nails cutting into the palms of her clenched hands, as they edged along. She didn't want to see familiar faces—familiar landmarks. She was being torn up by her roots, and it was hurting badly. Her future had seemed settled—secure—yet now it was in chaos, and she would have to go to some strange place, and begin all over again. But how could she? she asked herself in agony. Where could she go, and what could she do?

By the time they'd finally won free of the village, and were heading through the lanes towards the motorway, Lou's throat muscles were aching with misery, but she wouldn't allow herself to cry any more. Not yet. And certainly not in front of Alex Fabian.

As if he could read her thoughts, he said quietly, 'Things will get better. You are going to come through this.'

'I don't want to,' she said fiercely. 'I want my old life back.'

'Really?' His tone was caustic. 'You like skivvying for your family, do you? You enjoy being betrayed by people who are supposed to love you?'

'No,' she said. 'And stop making me sound like some kind of pathetic victim. After all,' she added, darting a burning glance in his direction, 'I'm not the only one who's been made a fool of.'

He sighed over-heavily. 'Sad, but true.'

Lou's lips tightened. 'I'm glad you can treat it all so lightly. To you, it's just a minor glitch on the surface of your untroubled life.'

'It's rather more than that,' he said. 'In fact, it's a major inconvenience, but I'll recover.'

'I'm sure you will,' she said with intense bitterness.

He sent her a faint smile. 'And, believe it or not, so will you—given time.' He paused. 'What are you going to do about your job? I presume you'll have to give notice.'

'It's normally a month,' she said tightly. 'But I have some holiday owing.' *Holiday that she'd hoped and planned to use for her honeymoon.* 'I—I'll write to the partners, and explain. I'm sure they'll understand—the circumstances…'

Her face worked suddenly, and all the tears she'd tried to dam back came welling inexorably to the surface again.

She said chokingly, 'Oh, no,' and pressed clenched fists to her streaming eyes.

Alex pulled the car into a convenient lay-by and stopped. Lou sat beside him, head bent, her shoulders shaking with the sobs she was trying hard to suppress. Even through the misery that overwhelmed her, she was aware of anger and shame at betraying herself like this in front of him.

She could only be grateful in a confused way that he did not look at her, or speak. Or touch her. That, she thought, most of all.

As she began to regain her self-control, however, she found herself being handed an immaculate white linen handkerchief.

'Thank you,' she mumbled. Then, stiffly, 'I'm sorry.'

'You don't have to apologise,' he said. 'Or explain.'

Lou mopped her face, and blew her nose. Still snuffling a little, she said, 'I'll have it laundered and returned to you.'

'Don't worry about it. I have plenty of others.' He closed the book of maps he'd been studying, and tossed it onto the rear seat. 'Shall we go on, or do you want to change your plans?'

The truth was she had no other plans, but she didn't want to admit that. She said, 'I'd just like to get to the farm, please.

I've already taken up too much of your time,' she added stiltedly.

'I can take the tears,' Alex said as he started the car. 'But not the humility. It's not your thing, darling. Just keep reminding yourself that I'm the heartless swine who's caused all your problems, and you'll be fighting fit in no time.'

She sent him one brief, fulminating glance, then transferred her attention ostentatiously to the passing hedgerow. Which was fine until they reached the motorway some fifteen minutes later, and all she had to stare at was other traffic.

'Why did you want to marry Ellie?' She'd meant to sit beside him in stony and unbroken silence for the duration, but curiosity eventually got the better of her.

'I didn't,' he said. 'I had no intention of getting married at all, but suddenly I needed a token wife, and Ellie seemed a likely candidate. That's all.'

'All?' Lou echoed, wonderingly. '*All?* How did Ellie feel about that?'

'Oh, she didn't want me either,' he said blandly. 'I—er—tested the waters quite early on to make sure.'

'Really.' She sent him an inimical glance. 'That must have hit you right in the ego.'

'On the contrary,' he returned, unmoved by her hostility. 'It convinced me that she was ideal for the part. After all, the last thing I wanted was someone who might fall in love with me.'

'Is this some weird, sophisticated game?' she asked coldly. 'Marrying people you don't give a damn about?'

'No, of course not,' he said. 'And I did give a damn about Ellie. While we were married I'd have made sure she got everything she could ever want in the way of comfort, plus a quick, no-fault divorce at the end of it all, with a generous settlement. Is that so bad a deal?'

'I'd say it was a cold-blooded nightmare.' Lou shook her head incredulously. 'I can't believe that Ellie would ever agree to such a thing.'

'But then,' he said softly, 'you didn't know Ellie as well as you thought—did you?' He let that sink in for a moment. 'And she certainly knew it was a business arrangement, and not a real marriage,' he added evenly. 'Although I admit we hadn't got around to discussing the small print.'

'No wonder she ran away,' Lou said bitterly. She was silent for a moment. 'But I still don't understand why you picked Ellie. You're a rich man. I'd have thought there would have been plenty of other more willing candidates around.'

'Too willing,' he said. 'That was the problem. Because they might not have wanted to leave after they'd outlived their usefulness.'

She said scornfully, 'Do you really think you're that irresistible?'

'I might be.' He slanted a swift grin at her. 'Under the right conditions.'

Well, she thought, biting her lip, she'd walked right into that.

She said coldly, 'To some women, perhaps. But not to me.' She paused again. 'If you really hate the idea so much, why get married at all?'

'I wouldn't,' he said. 'Only I'm being blackmailed.'

Lou became aware that her jaw had dropped, and hastily adjusted her face. 'By an irate husband, no doubt.'

'Wrong sex.'

'My God,' she said. 'Some woman you've refused to marry?'

'I doubt if she'd have me,' he said, deadpan. 'She'll be eighty-five in a few weeks, besides being my grandmother.'

'Your grandmother?' Lou echoed, then shook her head impatiently. 'Oh, I don't believe one word of all this. Are you involved in some insane practical joke?'

'I only wish I were,' he said, a note of grimness in his voice. 'Unfortunately it's no laughing matter. She wants me married, and she's in a position to apply pressure.'

'How?'

'By disinheriting me.'

'My God,' she said contemptuously. 'Are you really so desperate for cash? I thought you were supposed to be a wealthy man.'

'It's not a question of money.' His tone was curt. 'It's a house.'

She stared at him. 'And it means—that much to you?'

'I was born there,' he said. 'And so was my mother. I spent a lot of my childhood there, too, and I've always loved it—always known it would be mine one day.' He paused. 'And I'll do whatever it takes to ensure that it comes to me and no one else.'

'You mean that there's someone who could cut you out?'

'Some distant cousin,' he said, 'who's turned up from South Africa, complete with bride. And my grandmother has a bee in her bonnet about Rosshampton being a family house.' His mouth twisted. 'So, she's given me an ultimatum. Unless I put my neck on the wedding block, she's going to change the arrangements. Only I have no plans to change my way of life. Or not on any permanent basis.'

'You're saying you want someone to pretend to be your wife until your grandmother dies?' Lou said indignantly. 'But that's ghoulish.'

'Nothing of the kind,' Alex said briskly. 'For one thing, Selina has no intention of dying—ever. For another, she's always meant to make a gift of the house in her lifetime, to avoid death duties.'

'You have no compunction about making her give up her home?' she queried acidly.

'No one has ever made Selina do anything,' he returned. 'In any case, she finds life livelier in Holland Park these days,' he added sardonically. 'So ditch the image of the forsaken pensioner.'

She flushed. 'It's really none of my concern. But no wonder Ellie wanted nothing to do with such a crazy scheme. Who in her right mind would even consider it?'

'Actually,' Alex said calmly, 'I'm hoping that you might.'

Shock made it suddenly difficult to breathe. She twisted in her seat, staring at him in total incredulity, her flush spreading—burning over her entire body.

'You—have to be—joking,' she managed at last.

'On the contrary,' he said. 'I'm deadly serious. On your own admission, you need a job and a home. Step into Ellie's shoes, and I'll provide you with both. And as soon as Rosshampton belongs to me, you'll be completely free again, with a cash settlement, to go where you please, and make a new life. Is that really such a bad deal?'

'It's nauseating.' She was gasping. 'Monstrous.'

'A slight exaggeration,' he said. 'I prefer "practical". Because you must admit it would solve major problems for both of us. I'd have a wife to dangle in front of Selina. And you would have somewhere to lick your wounds. Get your head together again.'

She said thickly, 'Living with you? I don't think so.'

'But you wouldn't be living with me,' he said gently. 'Not in any real sense. We'd simply be sharing a roof. I thought I'd made that clear.'

He paused. 'You'd have all the space you need, Louise, with the added bonus that no one would feel sorry for you. Money has that effect.'

'You disgust me.'

'I'm sorry about that.' He sounded infuriatingly unmoved. 'I dare say your father will also have his regrets, now that the future of Trentham Osborne is seriously in question once more.'

'You mean you're going to cancel the re-financing?' Louise stared at the cool profile. 'But you can't do that.'

'Actually I can,' he said. 'Because it was always conditional.' He lifted a shoulder in a faint shrug. 'And the conditions are not being met.' He paused. 'You could, of course, change your mind—and persuade me to think again, too.'

There was an endless, tingling silence. Lou found she was counting the seconds in her head, as if she'd seen the lightning flash and was waiting for the inevitable crash of thunder.

At last, she said huskily, 'Your grandmother must be very proud of you. Where blackmail is concerned, you're a chip off the old block.'

'You don't have to accept my terms,' he said coolly. 'Considering the way your family appear to treat you, I think you'd be perfectly justified in allowing Trentham Osborne to go under.'

'But you know that I won't,' she said, bitterly. 'That I can't.'

'Yes,' he said. 'I know. In fact I was counting on it.' He shot her a swift glance, assimilating her pale, set face. 'So, you accept my proposition? You'll marry me—in name only? Until I get what I want?'

It was her turn to shrug, hunching a defensive shoulder. 'I don't seem to have a choice.'

'I'll take that as an acceptance of my honourable proposal.' He sounded amused. They were approaching a motorway junction. Before Lou knew what was happening, he'd signalled, changed lanes and was driving up the slip-road.

'What are you doing?' she demanded tensely. 'This isn't the exit we want. We're miles away.'

'Are your aunt and uncle expecting you?'

'No—not exactly…'

'Then we needn't trouble them,' Alex said, as he negotiated the roundabout. 'I think we should go straight back to London, and make the necessary arrangements.'

He paused. 'Under the circumstances, I suggest a special licence, and a private ceremony with just a couple of witnesses. Present our friends and relations with a *fait accompli*. What do you think?'

Her hands gripped each other so tightly in her lap that the knuckles turned white. 'You—you don't want to know what I think.'

He had the audacity to laugh. 'No—probably not.' He became brisk. 'We both missed breakfast, so I suggest we stop and have an early lunch. There's quite a good place a few miles from here.'

'I—I'm not hungry,' Lou denied swiftly.

'All the same, you need to eat.' He was civil but inexorable. 'You'll feel better after a meal.'

'I shall feel better,' she said, 'when your grandmother hands over the deeds of your precious house. And not before.' She shook her head. 'I still can't believe I'm doing this. It's madness.'

The restaurant he'd chosen was part of a country hotel set deep in its own grounds. There were a number of vehicles already parked on the gravel sweep that fronted the pillared portico, and Alex slotted his own car neatly into a vacant space.

'It's busy,' he commented. 'I'll go and make sure we can have a reservation.'

'It looks lovely,' Lou admitted, peering up at the mellow brick façade. 'I didn't even know it existed, so how did you find out about it?'

'I stay here sometimes, at weekends.' His tone was casual. 'It's comfortable, discreet, and the food is excellent.'

He was telling her obliquely that this was somewhere he brought his girlfriends, Lou realised, her face warming slightly, as he walked away. And no doubt he would continue to do so, after their farce of a wedding had taken place. He'd warned her, after all, that he was not going to alter his way of life.

And she didn't want him to, she hastily reminded herself. In fact, as far as she was concerned, he could take a different lady to a different hotel every weekend that their non-marriage lasted. Anything that would spare her his company had to be welcome.

He was only gone a few minutes, and when he returned he was holding a key card. 'I've taken a room for you,' he said. 'I thought you might like to freshen up a little—wash away the tear stains at least. I don't want people to think I've been ill-treating you.'

'Of course not,' she said. 'After all, what's a little blackmail and deception between friends?'

'I'm glad you consider us friends,' Alex said silkily. 'That's a step in the right direction at least.' He paused. 'Do you have a skirt in that bag of yours, because if so you might change into it?'

'No.' Lou faced him with a militant sparkle in her eyes. 'I don't. I was going to stay on a farm, remember.'

He shrugged. 'It doesn't really matter. You'll need a whole new wardrobe, anyway. We'll deal with that next week.'

'No,' she said, '*we* will not. If I need clothes, I'll buy them myself.'

'You're going to be dressing for a completely different life,' he said. 'And you're going to need guidance. Not negotiable,' he added swiftly, as her lips parted mutinously. 'Oh, and you can get rid of that band round your hair, too. I prefer it loose.'

Lou was quivering with temper. 'And why should I pay any attention to your preferences?'

'Because from now on, sweetheart, I'm calling the shots,' he said. 'And don't you forget it.' He gave her the key card. 'When you look less like an orphan of the storm, you can join me in the bar.' He paused. 'What can I get you, by the way?'

'If you're calling the shots,' Lou said icily, 'then you should know.' And she marched past him, up the shallow stone steps, and through the double glass doors, furiously aware that, if she looked back, she would find him laughing.

It was a beautiful room, she had to concede unwillingly, with its wide, canopied bed and elegant furniture. And the bathroom was the height of luxury with its gleaming tiles and marble surfaces. The roomy shower cubicle was constructed in a pretty hexagonal shape, and the tub was enormous, and clearly intended for dual occupation.

The perfect love nest, Lou thought with irony, inspecting the array of scented oils and lotions on offer as she dried her face and hands on one of the fluffy towels. Except that love would have very little to do with it.

For a brief moment she had a sharp, disturbing image of that bed in the other room occupied. Of Alex Fabian, his mouth smiling as he bent over some naked, sinuous beauty.

She closed her eyes swiftly, blotting the picture from her mind, bewildered at its sudden potency.

Wondering why she had thought of Alex and not David, who was probably entwined with his Ellie in a similar room somewhere.

She leaned against the cold edge of the marble for a moment, recovering her composure, then opened her eyes. She barely recognised the white, strained face looking back at her from the mirror. Her eyes were still slightly reddened, in spite of the cold water she'd splashed onto them, and her lips were pale and vulnerable.

Reluctantly she took her cosmetics purse from her bag, and made use of the concealer and compressed powder before adding a soft pink lustre to her unhappy mouth.

Finally, she took the band from her hair and shook it free, the dark, waving strands forming a silky aureole round her face.

It was a slightly braver picture than before, she thought, but no more than that. The inner fire which had once lit her eyes and flushed her cheeks had been quenched.

In just a few hours, she'd been transformed into a quiet grey shadow of her former self.

And no one in this world, especially a shrewd, manipulative old lady, was going to believe that she would ever be the choice of a man like Alex Fabian. Not in a month of Sundays. Because she hadn't even been enough for David, whom she'd loved.

Ellie, the golden, the glowing, would have convinced everyone, of course. And she would have enjoyed spending the money, and having clothes and jewellery lavished on her. She'd relished the glimpse of the high life that Alex had shown her, and she had the charm and prettiness to make her mark in the circles he moved in. She'd have made him a trophy wife, rather than the token variety.

He might even have fallen in love with her, given time, Lou thought, replacing her comb in her bag. But there had been no time. Instead there had been David…

She drew a deep, painful breath, then turned away from the mirror. It was time she went down to the bar before Alex came looking for her.

The long, low-ceilinged room was filled with people enjoying their aperitifs and looking at leather-bound menus, but she saw him at once, sitting at a table in the window, her gaze drawn to him like a magnet.

And she wasn't the only one. As she threaded her way to-

wards him, she was aware of other glances targeting him with
open avidity. Of women's fingers nervously playing with their
hair, their jewellery, as they watched him. Of laughter that was
pitched a fraction too high.

But why should she even be surprised? Alex Fabian was
always going to be a man who would attract female attention
without even trying, she thought. And he wasn't trying now,
just lounging on the cushioned seat, and staring out of the window.

He rose politely as she reached him, the cool eyes scanning
her, their expression unfathomable. 'Did you find everything
you needed?'

'Thank you—yes.' There were no spare chairs around, so
she took her place beside him on the window-seat, maintaining
a deliberate and cautious distance.

Alex lifted a hand in a silent signal, and a waiter appeared
from nowhere with an ice bucket containing a bottle of champagne, and two glasses.

Lou's brows drew together as she watched the man remove
the cork with a flourish and fill the glasses. 'What is this?' she
demanded in an indignant undertone, as soon as he'd departed.

'Bollinger,' Alex said. 'Conventional, I know, but we do
have our engagement to celebrate.'

'I fail to see why.'

'Then just regard it as a much-needed tonic,' he said softly.
'The wine for all seasons and all times of day.' He raised his
glass. 'To us.'

Then, as she made no move, he added mockingly, 'Or would
you prefer—absent friends?'

'No,' she said between her teeth, 'I would not.'

'Then choose your own toast,' Alex said. 'But drink to
something—anything. People are beginning to look.'

'Yes,' she said with quiet fierceness, 'because they're wondering what the hell you're doing with a—a nonentity like me.'
She took a deep breath. 'I'm sorry, but I've realised that I can't
do this after all. It just won't work. We—we wouldn't fool
anyone. Your grandmother will pick up in seconds that I'm not

in your league.' She swallowed. 'That we don't care for each other.'

He shrugged, his face suddenly hard. 'She specified marriage,' he countered. 'Not a love match. And it's too late for second thoughts, Louise. Our bargain stands. Now pick up your drink, and smile at me nicely for the audience. You need all the rehearsal you can get.'

The wine was cold and clear, the bubbles exploding in her head as she obeyed him.

And he smiled back at her, tiny, glittering devils dancing in his eyes, and reached for her hand, raising it to his lips and pressing a light, sensuous kiss into her palm.

Shock ran through her like a flame. She tried to snatch her hand back, but his clasp tightened.

'What—what do you think you're doing?' she demanded breathlessly.

'I felt the occasion called for a gesture,' Alex drawled. 'That was it.'

He paused, his gaze even as it met hers. 'Understand this, sweetheart. Whatever does not happen between us in private, in public we're the couple of the decade. I expect you to pretend—and pretend well.

'You will smile at me. You will not pull away when I touch you, or shudder if I should feel obliged to kiss you. You're getting well paid for a service, and that's the service you'll provide.

'And if you find physical contact between us difficult, then that's your problem,' he added with a touch of harshness.

She drank some more champagne quickly, trying to ignore the fact that her fingers were entwined with his, and that he was stroking the soft mound at the base of her thumb.

She said in a low voice, 'Is it—absolutely essential?'

'We'll be newly-weds. People will expect the occasional demonstration of affection. So what are you so uptight about?'

She took another frantic sip. 'Perhaps I'm not sure that—I can cope—with this kind of—intimacy.'

'Really?' His grin was cool and cynical. 'But I'm not irresistible, darling. You told me so yourself—remember?' He paused. 'However, if the going gets tough, just keep reminding yourself of the money. That should provide some consolation.'

'Yes,' Lou said softly and stormily. 'Because, one day, it will enable me to tell you to go straight to hell. And that will make it all worthwhile.'

'I'm sure it will,' he said silkily. 'And I'm also beginning to think that married life won't be nearly as dull as I expected.'

He allowed her to absorb that for a startled moment, then passed her a menu. 'Now—shall we order lunch?'

CHAPTER FOUR

LOUISE had ordered more or less at random, convinced that she would be unable to eat a thing, but discovered that the chilled cucumber soup and the perfectly poached salmon with its accompanying watercress salad were exactly what she wanted, and too delicious to resist anyway.

She found herself, somewhat defiantly, ordering a *crème brûlée* to follow.

Alex asked for cheese, after his choice of vegetable soup and rare roast beef sliced from the joint on the trolley.

Lou had to admit, as coffee was brought, that the meal hadn't been the nightmare she'd envisaged. Under other circumstances, she might even have found Alex pleasant company. He'd chatted lightly about the food, a film he'd seen, a book he'd recently read, a concert he'd attended, and while doing so, she realised afterwards, had managed to extract a fair amount of information about her own tastes.

They would never be lovers, they might not even be friends, but there was a faint possibility that they could manage a certain level of coexistence, she told herself, trying to feel hopeful.

'You're very quiet,' he said. 'I hope that's not a bad sign.'

'No.' She played with her coffee spoon. 'I was just—thinking.' She made herself look up, meet his quizzical gaze across the table. 'Thinking that I'll want the whole thing in writing—a proper contract between us.'

His brows lifted. 'Naturally,' he said with faint hauteur. 'Do you want your father's lawyers to act for you over the financial arrangements, or do you plan to conduct your own negotiations?'

'I—I wasn't talking about the money,' she said jerkily. 'But the rest of it. About it not being—a real marriage.'

'Ah,' he said meditatively. 'You mean you don't trust me to leave you in peace?'

'Not—precisely.' She drank some coffee. 'But I think it's better that the lines should be drawn. That we both know exactly where we stand.'

'About a thousand miles apart, by the sound of it.' He studied her with a faint frown. 'I have no plans to seduce you, Louise. I thought I'd made that clear.'

'Yes,' she said. 'But all the same...'

'All the same, you intend to hedge yourself round with rules and regulations,' he said softly. 'Tell me something, my sweet. Which of us don't you trust? Is it me? Or could it possibly be yourself?'

She bit her lip. 'Don't be ridiculous.'

'I ask,' he went on, 'because when I was holding your hand in the bar just now, your pulse was off the scale. And I found that—interesting.'

Lou put her cup down with a bang. 'You've never heard of stress?' she came back at him. 'I imagine I'm allowed some kind of reaction to the worst day of my entire life.'

'Or the first day of the rest of it,' he said equably, 'depending on your point of view.'

'Thank you,' she said. 'But the Pollyanna outlook has never appealed to me.'

'But if you're really so stressed,' he went on, 'the room is still ours for the rest of the afternoon, and I know something that might help.'

For a moment, the only sound to break the taut silence between them was her own indrawn breath. Then she rallied, her voice low and husky with anger.

'How dare you—how dare you even suggest...'

'A shoulder rub,' he supplied. 'It works for me every time.' He gave her a mocking grin. 'And I won't even make you take your clothes off—unless you insist, of course.'

Her throat muscles were tightening, and she was shaking inside, but she forced herself to lift her chin and confront him. She said, 'Kindly don't talk to me like that. Not now, not ever again, or the deal's off, and to hell with Trentham Osborne.'

'Hell,' Alex said, 'is going to be extremely crowded at this rate.' He paused. 'I suppose that's going to be Clause Three, subsection B of the contract. The party of the first part—me— will not tease, wind up or joke with the party of the second part—you. Especially on any subject even remotely connected with sex.'

She said stiffly, 'No doubt you find this very amusing…'

'No,' he said. 'I find it sad. But you're not the only woman in the world with a sense of humour bypass, so I'll get by.'

Lou saw just in time the pitfall in telling him in a dignified way that there was nothing wrong with her sense of humour.

She said coldly, 'Perhaps we could go now, please. The sooner we begin this nauseating charade, the sooner it will be over.'

'Not necessarily,' Alex said drily. 'But I catch your drift.'

His fingers clasped her arm lightly as they walked to the door.

'It's a statement,' Lou whispered silently, forcing herself not to flinch. 'Only a statement…'

And halted as she found their exit suddenly blocked.

'Why, Alex, darling.' The woman confronting them was beautiful, her vibrant red hair expertly layered, and the deep blue eyes fringed by impossibly long lashes.

She was wearing a knee-length black dress which hugged her spectacular figure, topped by a jacket in exaggeratedly large checks of black and white.

There were black onyx studs surrounded by pearls in her ears, and a matching pendant at her throat.

And the voice that issued from the smiling red lips was throaty and undeniably sexy. 'How utterly lovely to see you.'

'Lucinda,' Alex responded with cool civility. 'What a surprise to find you here.'

She laughed. 'Hardly, darling. This has always been one of my favourite places. And I rather fancied a trip down memory lane.'

'By yourself?'

'Of course not. Peter's parking the car. He's bribing me with lunch before we visit his elderly aunt. Practically gaga, but loaded.' A shrug. 'You know how it is.'

She turned her gaze to Louise, who found herself assessed and dismissed in one lightning glance. 'Aren't you going to introduce me to your friend?'

'To my fiancée, actually,' Alex drawled. 'Louise—this is Lucinda Crosby. Lucinda, I'd like you to meet Louise Trentham, who has just promised to become my wife.'

'Well,' Lucinda said softly, her eyes narrowing. 'How very surprising—and marvellous for you both, of course. And I thought…' She broke off artistically with a little laugh. 'My best wishes—and congratulations, especially to you, Alex, darling. I hope you'll be blissfully happy together.'

'I'm sure we shall.' Alex's arm slid round Lou's shoulders, and remained there. She felt herself quietly drawn against him, and fought the immediate impulse to resist.

Just another statement, she told herself. But this time she had the impression that it mattered.

It occurred to her at the same time that this was the closest she had ever been to him physically. That this was the kind of contact she would have to accustom herself to. And that it was never going to be easy.

The arm that held her was strong. The shoulder she leaned against was hard with muscle. She could smell the faint drift of some cologne he was wearing and feel the heat of his body through the layers of his clothing.

And in one blinding flash of revelation she knew exactly what the warmth—the scent of him would be like if he was naked and she was in his arms, naked too.

She felt the shock of that certainty deep in her bones—in the sudden surge of her blood. She felt the fine hairs rise along her spine, and her nipples harden helplessly against the thin wool of her sweater.

And thought, This is impossible. This *cannot* be happening to me.

Dazed, and trying desperately to hang on to her composure, she heard Lucinda say, 'But you're not rushing off, surely. You must wait for Peter, and then we can all have a drink together— to celebrate.'

'It's a kind thought,' Alex said smoothly. 'But perhaps some other time. We really have to go. We're getting married very soon, and we need to make a start on the arrangements. I'm sure you understand.'

'Of course.' Lucinda's smile widened. 'I shall be able to tell Peter all about your charming bride-to-be over lunch. I'm sure he'll be delighted for you.' She turned to Lou. 'Goodbye, my dear—Laura, is it?'

'Louise,' Lou supplied woodenly.

'Of course—and I'm Cindy. I know we're going to be great friends. Be sure and invite me to the wedding.'

Hell, Lou thought, smiling politely, will freeze over first— on both counts.

As they crossed the foyer to the reception desk, she was aware of the other woman's gaze boring into her back. She waited quietly while Alex paid the bill, getting herself back under control with a rigorous act of will, subduing her flurried breathing and the scamper of her pulses.

She could find no excuse or explanation for that totally animal reaction, and she was ashamed that she could be so easily beguiled. But it was one thing to recognise that Alex Fabian possessed a powerful sexuality. She'd known that since their first encounter. It was a different thing to find herself exposed to it—and at the mercy of her senses—when he hadn't even been trying.

Heaven help me if he ever did try, she thought, her mouth suddenly dry. Dear God, I shall have to be so very careful.

'Peter Crosby,' she said as they went out to the car. 'Isn't he in the government?'

'Yes.' His tone did not invite further enquiries.

Nor did she really need to ask. But something—some small, strange pain deep inside her—drove her on.

She said, 'Living in the country does not make me stupid, Alex.'

'I hope it doesn't make you over-curious about things that don't concern you either,' he returned curtly.

'No,' she said. 'You can live your life exactly as you wish. I can put that in the contract, too, if you like.'

'That,' he said, 'will not be necessary. And that particular episode is in the past, anyway.'

That's not what she thinks, Lou thought.

Aloud, she said, 'She met you with Ellie, didn't she?'

'She's met me with a lot of people.'

'And she meant me to know, didn't she? That you'd stayed here together?'

'God knows,' he said. 'Possibly. Probably. I never figured out how Lucinda's mind worked.'

'But then,' she said, 'I don't suppose her mind was ever her chief attraction.'

'Ouch.' He sounded amused. 'You have sharp claws, country mouse.'

And I suspect I'm going to need them, Lou thought as they drove off.

It was a quiet journey. Alex found a classical channel on the radio, and she lay back, eyes closed, letting the music wash over her, deliberately making her mind a blank.

She did not want to contemplate what lay ahead of her in London. She did not want to think about the choice she had made, or the risks she was taking. And how serious those risks were had become only too apparent in the past hour.

The past was too painful to remember. The future was a leap in the dark. It was better to let herself drift. She might even have dozed a little.

But Alex's voice telling her quietly that they were coming into London brought her sharply back to full awareness of the difficult present.

She struggled to sit upright, pushing her hair back from her face, hoping that her mouth hadn't dropped open, or that she hadn't—oh, God—been snoring.

She cleared her throat. 'I—I've just realised that I've no idea where I'm being taken. A hotel, I suppose.'

He said, 'We're going to my flat.'

'Oh?' She stiffened. 'Why?'

'Because we have a lot to talk about,' he said. 'And being under the same roof makes conversation easier, somehow.'

'Yes,' she said, 'I—I see that. It's just that I didn't expect to move in with you before—the marriage.'

'For God's sake.' He was half amused, half exasperated. 'I'm not asking you to share a bedsit. There are two bedrooms in the damned place, and the doors lock.'

He paused. 'And it's the norm for lovers to live together. It might be found extraordinary if we didn't.'

She swallowed. 'We are not—lovers.'

'In the eyes of the world we are. So carried away by our feelings, in fact, that we can't wait to tie the knot. You might care to remind yourself of that from time to time,' he added sardonically. 'It could add depth to your performance.'

'Did you take Ellie there?' She couldn't remember it ever being mentioned.

'I hardly had the opportunity,' Alex drawled. 'No sooner had she agreed to marry me than she was disappearing over the horizon. But I planned to show her the place—ask if she was prepared to live there. After all, she might have hated it.'

Lou lifted her chin. 'And I might too.'

'Of course,' he said. 'And if so, you must tell me, and we'll start house-hunting. Find something that will suit you better.'

She gasped. 'You mean you'd be prepared to give up your home for this—non-relationship?'

'Firstly,' he said, 'it's not my home in any real sense. It's just a flat. The only place I care for, as I've made clear, is Rosshampton. Which is why we're involved in this "non-relationship", as you so eloquently describe it.

'Secondly, you're doing me an immense favour,' he added levelly. 'And the least I can do in return is make sure that you're as happy as I can make you, which includes your immediate surroundings.'

'Well,' Lou said awkwardly, 'thank you—I think.'

'I have to tell you,' he said, 'that after your stepsister's wide-eyed compliance with everything I said and did, you come as something of a shock to the system, Miss Louise Trentham.'

She hunched a shoulder. 'Don't despair, Mr Fabian. I may dwindle into compliance myself, given time, and the gratification of my every wish. And Ellie wasn't the pushover you thought, either.'

'I stand corrected,' he said, the ghost of a laugh in his voice.

She hated it when he did that, because it made her want to smile back at him.

'So what else does this flat have besides its two bedrooms with the lockable doors?' She made herself sound brisk and businesslike.

'Two bathrooms, a dining room, and a drawing room with a balcony which leads up to a private roof garden, where you can sunbathe in the nude if you wish.'

'I don't,' Lou said coldly. 'But I gather that makes your flat the penthouse. I suppose I should have guessed.'

'You make me feel as if I've failed some basic test.' The amusement in his tone deepened. 'Besides, someone has to live up there, and I thought the garden might actually appeal to you. It has some nice tubs and things.'

'Sent round from Harrods each spring, no doubt,' Lou said. 'I can't see you up to your elbows in compost.' She paused. 'You didn't mention a kitchen.'

'There is one,' he said. 'I'm almost sure I've seen it.'

'But it doesn't get much use.'

'The kettle works,' he said. 'And the microwave. And I have an excellent corkscrew.'

'Well,' she said, 'what more could one want?'

'But then,' he said, gently, 'you'd hardly expect me to spend my leisure hours grinding up pesto, or perfecting my soufflé.'

Lou found she did not want to consider how Alex Fabian

might occupy his leisure. She said rather hurriedly, 'Do you have a housekeeper?'

'No, because the flat is fully serviced. The maid comes in every day, and laundry and dry-cleaning is back in twenty-four hours. There's a gym, sauna and swimming pool in the basement, underground parking, and a good restaurant on the first floor, which also delivers.' Alex sent her a lightning glance. 'Am I selling you the idea?'

'It sounds quite attractive,' she admitted sedately.

'You overwhelm me.'

'Oh, no,' she said. 'I don't aspire to that.' She considered. 'I think I'm going to aim to be unobtrusive. If I move into the kitchen, we'll probably never meet at all.'

'Let's cling to that thought.' He spoke cordially, but there was an odd note in his voice, almost like suppressed anger.

And that, thought Lou, was ridiculous.

Part of her wanted to hate the flat, but she couldn't. It was too spacious, and the views from its windows too spectacular. It had soft carpets, subdued lighting and furniture to sink into.

But it certainly wasn't a home. Alex had been right about that. It looked as if it had been tastefully assembled by a good designer, she thought, looking round her, but there were no personal touches. Nothing to give a clue to the character of the owner. Even the flower arrangement in the hall looked as if it was too correct to shed a petal.

'What do you think?' Alex propped himself in the doorway of the drawing room, watching her move round.

'You don't spend much time here, do you?'

'No,' he said. 'I thought you'd find that a point in its favour. But can you bear to live in it?'

She bit her lip. 'Yes,' she said. 'As far as the situation itself is bearable.

'Then perhaps you'd like to come and look at the bedrooms. Decide which one you want.' He paused. 'At present, I'm using the master bedroom myself, but if that's the one you'd prefer I'll move out. It's not a problem.'

'No,' Lou said hastily. Even if he moved to another planet, it would still be his bed she was using, and the mere thought made her throat tighten. 'The other one will be fine,' she added with an attempt at lightness. 'It's not important, after all. Just a place to sleep in.'

'As you say,' Alex agreed rather too gravely. 'So shall we just toss a coin?'

'No.' She smiled resolutely. 'There's no need. I'll have the spare bedroom.'

'Very well.' He picked up her bag, and started down the passage. He threw open a door, then stood aside to allow her to precede him.

It was a large room, with tall windows hung with long cream curtains. The tailored bedspread on the wide bed was cream also, and the carpet was a soft blue.

'The bathroom's there.' Alex pointed. 'And the door next to it is the dressing room, although it's more of a walk-in closet.' He looked around him, grimacing slightly. 'It's very much a guest room, isn't it? I hadn't realised.'

'Well,' Lou said, 'I'm a guest.'

'Look,' he said, 'do whatever you like with it. Have it re-decorated—change the furniture—anything you want.'

'There's really no need,' she said. 'I shan't be staying that long.'

'I can't guarantee that,' he said. 'There's no set time limit. My grandmother is a law unto herself, and she'll act when she's ready, and not before. In the meantime, there's no reason why you shouldn't be comfortable.'

'I shall be.' Lou squared her shoulders. 'It's actually a very nice room.' She hesitated. 'Where do you sleep?' She tried to sound casual.

'Across the passage.' He indicated the door behind him, and gave her a quizzical look. 'I hope that's a sufficient distance.'

This time her hesitation was fatal, and his brows snapped together.

'Clearly not,' he commented coldly. 'And I'm beginning to find the role of potential rapist a little wearing. I wonder what they did with the stones from the Berlin Wall. I could find a use for them.'

Lou bit her lip. 'I'm sorry,' she said with constraint. 'I didn't mean…' She stumbled to a halt. 'This isn't easy for me.'

'It isn't what I'd have chosen either,' Alex came back at her, his frown deepening. 'I didn't realise I'd be sharing my life with a professional virgin. No wonder your fiancé cleared out. You must have frozen him away.'

'You—bastard.' Lou almost choked on the word, wrapping her arms defensively round her body. 'Don't you dare say that. I loved David, and I wanted him—wanted to belong to him.'

'Then why didn't you?' he challenged. 'Instead of—saving yourself for marriage like some Victorian miss.'

'We agreed to wait. It was a mutual decision.' She drew a deep breath. 'And anyway, it's not that easy, not in a village where everyone knows everyone else's business. Besides, there was his mother…'

'Those are excuses—not reasons,' he said. 'There are ways and means. You could have gone away together somewhere. That hotel where we had lunch—how many of those couples do you think were married?'

She gasped. 'You think that's what I wanted? To be taken off for some—sordid weekend?'

'Why should it be sordid,' he said, 'if you love each other? Why couldn't it be passionate, and exciting—and fun?'

'You speak from the depth of your own vast experience, of course,' she said scornfully. 'But I'm talking about real love. The sort that lasts a lifetime—not casual sex with other people's partners. So don't lecture me about love, because you—you don't know the meaning of the word.'

'Perhaps not,' he said slowly. 'But I know there's an imperative that drives men and women together through fire and flood. And your romance sounds a pretty tepid affair to me. Perhaps David thought so too. Perhaps he wanted more than safety and domesticity, and sex on Friday nights when there was an ''r'' in the month.'

'You have no right to say these things.' Lou flung her head back. 'No right at all.'

'No,' he said unexpectedly, 'I haven't. But maybe someone needs to tell you a few home truths about this deathless love of yours, before you wrap it round you like a security blanket and end up strangling in it. Because there's no safety in love. It's the ultimate risk, not a soft option with a wedding ring and roses round the door.'

'Have you—quite finished?'

'Almost.' He paused, then said more gently, 'It's probably too late to say I didn't mean to hurt you, but it's true. Maybe I shouldn't have said what I did. But the fact is they made fools of us both. And it riles me to think that neither of them had the guts to stand up and admit what was going on. Tell us to our faces that they wanted more than we had to offer. And in your heart, you must feel that too.'

She stared at him. 'Don't you dare tell me what's going on in my heart.' Her voice rose stormily. 'You know nothing about me—nothing.'

'You're right,' he said, 'I don't. But during the course of our short marriage, I plan to find out.' He turned away. 'I'll leave you to unpack.'

'What makes you think I'll stay here another minute?' she flung after him.

Alex sighed. 'Louise—you have nowhere else to go. And we have a deal.' The green eyes were cool, direct and implacable. 'Stay with me—marry me—and Trentham Osborne get another chance. Otherwise they don't. Jobs will be lost. Good books will not be published, and your father and his wife will lose their home. But it's entirely up to you. As it always was.'

He glanced at his watch. 'I'm going out for a while. If you're still here when I return our deal goes ahead, with no more arguments or recriminations. A business decision, no more, no less. So, think about it.'

The door closed behind him.

Lou sank down on the edge of the bed, still hugging herself protectively, staring ahead of her with eyes that saw nothing.

The silence pressed down on her, surrounded her. She was shaking inside, her mind in freefall.

He was vile, she thought. Vile, disgusting and heartless. The things he had said seared her memory, and she would never forgive him—never.

But, at the same time, she could not ignore the tiny voice in the corner of her mind that whispered he was right. That her relationship with David was never strong enough to stay the course. That if they had loved ardently enough, nothing could have kept them apart. That what she'd thought was consideration had merely been a warning signal that all was not well.

After all, he had had no such qualms about running away with Ellie, she acknowledged sadly.

Her overwhelming impulse was to pick up her bag, and leave. Find a hotel for the night, then make her way to Paddington in the morning. She could be at the farm by lunchtime. And Alex Fabian would not follow her. He'd made that clear.

If she left—it was over. And the fate of Trentham Osborne would be sealed. And, as her father had said, they would lose everything. Undoubtedly, both the London flat and Virginia Cottage had been used as collateral to raise money in the past, and would be snatched away if the company collapsed.

And, while she might not have had the easiest of relationships with Marian and her father, she could not wish to see them destitute—especially when she had the power to prevent it.

And when Alex Fabian had achieved his purpose, she would be totally free to do whatever she wished—go wherever she wanted.

Machu Picchu, she thought. Ayers Rock. The temples of Cambodia. So many places in the world that she'd thought she would never see, because David wasn't keen on foreign travel. And soon she would have the time and the money to explore them all.

If her life had to change, then she would make sure it was a change for the better.

She would earn Alex Fabian's money, she told herself with steely determination. Earn it—and ultimately enjoy it, in the certain knowledge that she would never have to set eyes on him again.

And she would not come cheap. He would pay, and pay again for her services. He might even be sorry their paths had ever crossed.

She got to her feet and took her bag into the dressing room, which had one wall lined with shelving and drawers, and another occupied by fitted wardrobes. Her few belongings looked lost and lonely in all that space. Rather as she herself felt, she thought wryly, then paused.

That was negative thinking, and whatever happened she was going to emerge from this situation as a victor not a victim.

And tried to ignore that small, aggravating voice now whispering an insistent reminder that Alex Fabian was someone who also expected to win. And generally succeeded.

She said aloud, 'But not this time.' And made it sound like a vow.

CHAPTER FIVE

LOUISE was sitting curled up in a corner of a sofa, trying hard to concentrate on the paperback thriller she'd brought with her, when Alex returned several hours later.

She raised her head slowly, and looked at him standing motionless in the doorway, aware that her heart was thudding unevenly. And that it had occurred to her more than once that he might not come back at all...

There was a long silence, then he said quietly, 'Thank you.'

'Don't be too grateful,' she returned with an assumption of coolness. 'I fully intend to take you to the cleaners.'

'I can accept that.' He walked to the sofa opposite, removing his jacket and tossing it over the padded arm. 'And I'm sure it will be very good for my soul.'

He leaned back against the cushions, closing his eyes briefly. For the first time since she'd met him, he looked weary—even strained—and Louise had detected the faint tang of whisky as he walked past her.

She said, 'Where have you been?'

'That's a very wifely question, darling,' he drawled. 'Getting into your role already?'

'Isn't that what you wanted?'

'Of course.' He opened his eyes and met her gaze. 'Actually, I walked for a while, and then I went to the bank, and did some work.'

'At this time—on a Saturday?' Her voice lifted in disbelief.

'Why not? I've never been a nine-to-five man, and I like to know I won't be interrupted. Besides, there were some things I needed to get out of the way.' He paused. 'I called your father, and told him that the re-financing of Trentham Osborne would go ahead as arranged.'

'You did?' Louise's eyes widened in bewilderment. 'But how did you know I'd still be here?'

'I didn't.' His tone was laconic. 'I just decided that if you were going to stay, I'd rather it was of your own accord rather than any threat I could hold over you.' He paused. 'Which, in turn, means that you're free to leave, if you want, and I won't stop you.'

She swallowed. 'That's—good of you. But I've decided to remain—to stick to my side of the deal, as agreed.' She hesitated. 'Did you tell my father where I was?'

'Yes.' She detected a faint chill. 'I told him.'

'What did he say?'

Alex shrugged, his mouth twisting. 'He seemed to take it in his stride.'

Louise bit her lip. 'I expect he was too relieved about the company to understand properly.'

'That's certainly the charitable way of looking at it,' he said drily. 'I wonder what he'll do next time he needs a daughter to sacrifice.'

She bent her head. 'Has there been any word,' she asked in a low voice, 'from Ellie?'

'Apparently not,' Alex returned. 'But plenty of words from the bridegroom's mother, who's been haunting the place all day, having acute hysterics. As a result, your stepmother has retired to bed with a severe migraine.'

'Oh, poor Marian.' Louise found herself suppressing a giggle. 'I can imagine. Mrs Sanders is the ultimate monster.'

'Then she should find Virginia Cottage a home from home,' Alex retorted caustically. He shook his head. 'How the hell did you ever get lumbered with such completely selfish relations?'

'We just inhabit different worlds, that's all.' Louise moved uncomfortably. 'And I think I remind my father too much of my mother.' She sighed. 'He's always felt guilty, I'm sure, that he wasn't there when she died—among other things.'

'And handing you over to me will somehow assuage his guilt?' There was a scornful note in his voice.

'I don't know,' she said. She tried to muster a smile. 'But it will certainly get me out of the way.'

'So,' he said, 'what made you decide to keep to our bargain, after all?'

She shrugged. 'As you've pointed out, I'm homeless and jobless.' She lifted her chin. 'I need the money you're going to pay me to kick-start my life all over again.'

He linked his hands loosely behind his head as he watched her. 'And how do you propose to do that?'

'Well,' she said, 'first, I shall go round the world. And when I've done that, I shall come home and train properly for a career.'

'In the law?'

'Perhaps,' she said. 'Or teaching. I shan't decide anything immediately.' Her smile was wintry. 'I have to survive the next few weeks and months before that.'

'You might, of course, fall in love and get married instead.'

'Oh, no.' Louise shook her head with determination.

'You seem very positive about it.' His voice was faintly amused.

'While you were out, I had a lot of time to think—about what you said to me earlier about my affair with David being…tepid.'

He moved sharply, almost defensively. 'If you remember, I did apologise for that.'

'Yes, but it occurred to me there could be an element of truth in it, all the same. That maybe David started seeing me because we were the right age, and knew the same people, and it was—convenient. But that's not good enough—is it? I should have realised when he kept finding excuses not to make the engagement official, or fix a date for the wedding.'

She smiled wanly. 'It was all supposed to be out of consideration for his mother, but I bet he hasn't given her a second thought since he left.'

He said quite gently, 'Louise, don't punish yourself like this.'

'Is that what I'm doing? I thought I was being realistic.

Facing up to a few things.' Her hands gripped each other in her lap. 'And just think how much worse it would all have been if we'd been properly engaged—or even married.'

He shrugged. 'Nothing lasts forever—least of all marriage, these days,' he added cynically.

'Mine would have lasted,' she said. 'I'd have made it work.'

'How ferocious you sound.' His own voice held amusement. 'And now you can concentrate all that determined will of yours on the job in hand—pretending to be my wife in front of my grandmother.'

She stared down at her clenched hands. 'Couldn't we keep it like that—just a pretence, rather than actually getting married? It would make things so much easier—later on. When it's all finished with.'

'Alas, no.' Alex gave a wry shrug. 'If I know Selina, she'll demand to see the marriage certificate. There has to be a wedding, but it will be quick, quiet, and as painless as I can make it.'

'Yes.' She bit her lip. 'Actually, I thought that was where you might have gone—to see your grandmother, to tell her...'

'She's not around.' He smiled faintly. 'Every year at this time she goes on a kind of royal progress to visit all those of her friends who are still standing. You'll have to wait to meet her at her birthday party—at Rosshampton.'

His voice seemed to caress the word.

Oh, God, Louise thought. This means so much to him. Suppose it all goes horribly wrong.

He was speaking again, more briskly. 'Have you learned your way round the flat yet?'

'As much as I need to do.' She forbore to mention that his bedroom had been the only no-go area. 'You certainly weren't joking about the kitchen. The cupboard's bare—and the fridge.'

'Damnation,' he said. 'You've had nothing to eat. I should have shown you how to use the internal phone—order from the restaurant. Would you like them to bring up some sandwiches?'

'Oh, no, I'm fine,' she assured him hastily. She paused.

'Would you mind if I got some food in—stocked up a bit on basics?'

His brows lifted. 'Trying to domesticate me already, darling?'

'I was thinking of stuff like milk and bread,' Louise said steadily. 'Not dinner for two.'

He shrugged. 'This is your home for the duration,' he said. 'Buy whatever you need. Just make sure there are always plenty of my favourite coffee beans, as well as your herbal stuff.'

'I'm not totally committed to camomile,' she said lightly. 'Sometimes I ring the changes with hot chocolate.' She got to her feet. 'If you don't mind, I'd like to go to my room now.' She tried to smile. 'It's been—quite a day.'

'And this,' he said softly, 'is only the beginning.'

He rose too, and she had to control an impulse to step back. 'Have you everything you need?'

'Oh, yes,' she said quickly. 'I'm sure I'll be very comfortable.'

'Well, if you think of anything, let me know,' he said. 'I'm going to watch television for a while.'

There *was* something, of course. The lock on her door had no key, after all, but she felt, absurdly, that this was not the most appropriate moment to mention it.

It can wait till morning, she told herself.

'Fine.' She sounded cheerful to the point of inanity, she realised crossly. 'Goodnight, then.'

'Sleep well,' he said, smiling faintly. 'And—sweet dreams.'

Unlikely, Louise thought as she escaped. Although screaming nightmares were a definite possibility.

Her head was aching slightly, and her eyes still felt sore from weeping as she let herself into her room. She had no aspirin with her, but maybe a hot bath would take away some of the stress.

It wasn't going to be acting a part in front of his grandmother which was going to present the major difficulty, she acknowledged as she began to run water into the tub, adding a splash of the lily-scented bath oil which stood with the array of other expensive toiletries on the tiled surround. It was the ordinary day-to-day living under the same roof. Trying not to jump when he entered the room, or overreacting whenever he came within three yards of her.

I wish, she thought drily, that there was a crash course I could take in becoming used to having him around.

I'd really like to be able to take it as easily for granted as he does himself. Although, of course, he's had infinitely more practice.

And found herself grimacing at the thought with something very like real pain.

The bath helped. She lay back in the warm, fragrant water, eyes closed, her head resting on the small pillow provided for the purpose, letting herself drift above the confusion of emotion within her. Telling herself there would be a time when none of it would matter any more. And hoping desperately that it was true.

She dried herself slowly on one of the thick, luxurious bath sheets, then rubbed creamy, scented body lotion into her skin before putting on the simple white lawn gown with its low-cut bodice and narrow straps, which was the only nightdress she'd brought with her.

Altogether too bridal, she thought, pulling a critical face at her reflection. Red flannel pyjamas would have been more appropriate.

She felt relaxed but not particularly drowsy as she climbed into bed, so she piled the pillows behind her and reached for her book. Considering she'd been reading it for most of the evening, she could remember very little of the plot, she thought, turning back to the beginning again.

She'd just started the second chapter when she heard it. The quiet but definite sound of a knock on her door.

The book slipped from her hands. 'Who—who is it?' she called, her voice strangled.

'Who do you think?' He sounded irritable rather than

amorous, she noted thankfully. 'There's hardly a cast of thousands out here. May I come in?'

'I'm in bed.' It was a feeble protest and she knew it.

'Really—in a bedroom?' His tone was caustic. 'How bizarre. This I must see.'

The door opened, and he walked in, carrying a tray on which reposed a steaming porcelain beaker. And a plate of biscuits.

Louise's eyes widened incredulously. 'What is this?'

'You said you liked hot chocolate.' He placed the tray on the night table. 'I ordered some for you.'

'Oh,' she said, touching the tip of her tongue to dry lips. 'That was—kind.'

'Well, make the most of it.' He slanted a grin at her. 'It doesn't happen very often. It's also practical,' he added. 'Lunch was a long time ago, and you could have problems trying to sleep on an empty stomach.'

'Yes,' she said. 'Yes—I suppose so.'

'Is the bed all right?' He tested the mattress with an experimental hand, then sat down on its edge. 'I've never slept in it.'

Well, that at least was a comfort, Louise thought, her apprehension increasing with every second. She tried unobtrusively to move further back against her pillows.

'And I've no immediate plans to do so,' he went on mockingly. 'Unless you insist, which seems unlikely. I hope that sets your mind at rest.'

'I'm really not concerned.' She tried to sound nonchalant. 'I hardly think you'd be stupid enough to jeopardise our deal.'

'No,' he said, 'but—to seal it perhaps.' And he leaned forward and kissed her lightly but sensuously on her parted lips.

She wanted to leap away, shuddering—to scream her outrage—to hit and claw at him, but that would only suggest that it was important to her. That it mattered too much. And she could not let him think that.

So by a superhuman effort she forced herself to remain still and passive under his brief, but telling, exploration of her mouth.

And when, at last, he lifted his head and looked at her, his green eyes shadowed and speculative, she spoke with cool derision. 'Just testing the waters again, Mr Fabian?'

'As you say, Miss Trentham,' he murmured. 'And they were just as icy as I expected—and as you could wish.'

She said crisply, 'I'm delighted to hear it—if it means I'll be spared any more of your unwanted advances.' She turned, and gave one of her pillows a thump. 'And now, if I could have some privacy?'

And only realised as she saw his gaze sharpen and focus that her sudden movement had caused the thin strap of her nightgown to slip down from her shoulder, revealing, as it did so, far too much of the rounded curve of her breast.

Alex tutted reprovingly, then leaned forward and hooked a finger under the errant strap, lifting it back into place with exaggerated solicitude, breathing in, as he did so, with smiling and quite deliberate appreciation, the warm fragrance of her skin.

'Careful, darling,' he said softly, 'or I might think you were coming on to me—and that would never do. Would it?'

He got to his feet and sauntered to the door, whistling quietly under his breath. Then turned.

'Enjoy your chocolate,' he said, and disappeared.

Her hand was already reaching for the tray, to send his damned chocolate crashing after him, when some instinct halted her. Warned her that was just what he'd be expecting. And that, more than anything else, she needed to keep her cool.

To demonstrate her total indifference to the kiss that still seemed to be burning on her lips—and to that stroking, too-knowing finger that had left its indelible brand on the bare skin of her shoulder. To his intimate enjoyment of the scent she'd rubbed into the smoothness of her skin.

Not shaken, she thought, ignoring the fact that her heartbeat was going crazy. Not stirred, either, in any way that he would ever discover.

Because Alex Fabian was a sexual predator *par excellence*.

One sign of weakness—one drop of blood in the water—and he would be circling on her. Moving in for the kill.

She could no longer doubt that he believed it would happen. Not immediately, as he'd said himself. But eventually. Not 'if' but 'when'...

When time and enforced proximity had done their work.

When the ring on her finger, allied to the indisputable fever in her blood, gave her no reason to resist him any longer.

Because, she realised with an odd sense of detachment, he would make her want him. He had that power, as she'd probably recognised in the first moments of their meeting. Recognised and feared...

And, if she was honest, the lingering touch of his mouth on hers had already done its damage. Because there had been a brief, shocking moment when she'd felt the sharp pang of desire. When she'd longed for more, and it would have been so easy to put her arms round his neck and draw him down to her. So easy—and so fatal, she thought, shivering.

She swallowed. Well, if he was the irresistible force, she would have to be the immovable object, adamant and unyielding in spite of him. Keeping him rigidly at much more than arm's length.

And causing him to experience failure for once in his spoiled, self-indulgent life. A rejection that would register on the Richter scale for a man who regarded women as his legitimate prey.

Because it was nothing more than a game to him, she acknowledged bitterly, and one that he confidently expected to win. Her inexperience would be a challenge to him, and he'd regard seduction as a bonus while he set out to acquire the house of his dreams.

Pass 'Go', she thought, her mouth curling, and collect whatever was available.

Only she wasn't playing. She was deadly serious. And she wasn't available either.

Alex Fabian was her ticket to the new life she needed to build for herself. But that was all he was, she cautioned herself.

And she could not allow herself to consider him in any other way.

Otherwise, she would just be another name on the long list of sad women who'd mistaken his lovemaking for love.

Not, she thought sorrowfully, that she knew a great deal about love either, or she would not be here now—a puppet dancing to Alex Fabian's strings…in every way but one.

And tomorrow she would start again—guarded, wary. Armoured against the involuntary pull of her senses in response to his wickedly male allure.

And, in the meantime, she still had the solace of hot chocolate and biscuits. A much safer consolation at bedtime, she told herself, her mouth twisting wryly, as she leaned across to reach for the beaker.

And noticed for the first time the metallic glint of what was lying beside it. A key. *The* key to her bedroom door, in fact.

And offered, she thought with sudden fury, in the full and certain knowledge that her pride would not allow her to use it. That she would use her own force of will to keep him away, rather than cowering behind locks and bolts.

And that what had happened between them was merely a preliminary skirmish, with the real battle to follow.

'So be it, then,' she said aloud, her voice shaking. 'I'm ready for you.'

And, for no reason she could ever explain, she burst into tears.

When she awoke the next morning, she felt drained and almost disorientated. But maybe that last bout of weeping had been exactly what she needed, because she seemed to have slept deeply and dreamlessly.

Overslept, in fact, she realised, glancing at her watch. And she had better get up and dress before Alex came to find her.

She showered rapidly, then dragged on close-fitting cream trousers that hugged her slim hips and long legs, topping them with a matching crew-neck sweater.

As she walked along the passage to the sitting room, she

realised that her hands were balled tensely into fists, and thrust them into the concealment of her pockets.

Alex was lounging on one of the sofas, reading the financial pages of one of the Sunday broadsheets, a cup of coffee beside him, the paper's remaining sections scattered at his bare feet.

He was wearing, Louise saw with a nervous leap of her pulse, a black silk robe, and apparently nothing else. His tawny hair was still damp from the shower, and she was breathlessly aware of the faint scent of some enticing citrus-based fragrance in the air.

He said, without looking up, 'Good morning. There's more coffee in the kitchen if you'd like some, although you'll have to take it black.'

'It doesn't matter.' She needed a shot of caffeine to energise her. Get her focused. Also an excuse to get away from the sight of all that brown, muscular chest and long, tanned legs exposed by the inadequacies of his dressing gown.

This, presumably, was how he chose to spend his Sunday mornings, she thought with a mental shrug. And he was signalling quite clearly that her presence would not change a thing.

When she returned, he was putting down the white internal phone.

'I've ordered scrambled eggs and smoked salmon to be delivered in about fifteen minutes. I hope that suits you.'

'Yes—thank you.' She hesitated. 'But it seems crazy to order something from a restaurant that I could easily make for us both.'

'Wanting to cook for me, darling?' He came back to his seat, shaking his head reprovingly. 'That's the first step on the slippery slope. Next, you'll be offering to have my babies.'

'No,' Louise said between her teeth, 'I will not.'

'I'm relieved to hear it,' he murmured unabashed, and continued his scrutiny of the paper.

When the scrambled eggs arrived, they were accompanied by Buck's Fizz, brown toast, curls of butter in a small dish and

Seville marmalade. And a further tall pot of coffee, with, this time, a jug of cream.

Louise, discovering she was ravenous again, ate and drank everything she was offered.

Breakfast over, she said stiltedly, 'Can you tell me where I'll find the nearest supermarket?'

'No,' he said. 'But my driver will undoubtedly know. If you can curb your housewifely impulses for twenty-four hours, I'll send him to pick you up tomorrow.'

'Is that strictly necessary?'

'You'll certainly find it more convenient.' He paused. 'Do you plan to question everything I say?'

Louise flushed. 'I'm just not used to having my decisions made for me.'

He shrugged. 'Then that's something you'll have to deal with. Although I promise to try and curb my natural arrogance,' he added drily. 'And any—suggestions I make are only intended for your benefit. Why struggle with buses or cope with the rush-hour on the underground when you don't have to?'

Louise's mouth tightened in irritation. 'How do you always manage to sound like the voice of sweet reason?' she asked crisply.

He grinned at her. 'Years of practice. And as you're cross anyway, may I wind you up further by suggesting that you turn your mind to forgetting the past, and start looking forward to the future?'

'Not easy,' she said, 'when I've no real idea when I'll be free to enjoy it.'

'Then don't think about that aspect,' Alex said softly. 'Concentrate instead on the prospect of seeing the Taj Mahal at sunset, or exploring the Great Barrier Reef.'

'And what do I do about the current situation?' She lifted her chin. 'Simply—grit my teeth?'

'I don't think a bride with her jaw permanently set would give a convincing picture of wedded bliss,' he said reflectively. 'You'll need to do better than that.'

'How much better?' Her tone held misgiving.

He considered for a moment. 'Primarily, you need to relax more. At the moment you're vibrating like some high-tension cable whenever I'm around.'

It might help if you were actually wearing some proper clothes. She permitted the thought, but didn't dare utter it aloud. Because she could not let him see that anything he said or did mattered. Or that his lack of attire allied with the beguilingly clean scent of his skin had the least effect on her.

She drew a breath. 'So what do you want me to do?'

The green eyes studied her dispassionately. 'You need to be able to smile, to walk with your arm in mine, and to talk without spitting my name out like cobra venom. At some point at my grandmother's party we'll be expected to dance together, without you turning to stone in my arms.'

He paused. 'And, of course, we're going to have to kiss each other as if we meant it,' he added silkily. 'To behave, in fact, as if we were physically and mentally attuned.'

She said harshly, 'The perfect couple.'

'You've got it in one,' he returned coolly. 'Pretend it's the next production of your village drama group, darling, with costumes and script supplied, and you'll be fine.' He studied her rigid expression, his mouth twisting wryly. 'And in return I promise to keep the kisses to a minimum, although I suspect the opposite course of action might yield better results.'

'On the contrary.' She took a quick, uneasy breath, anxious to move the conversation to safer ground. 'Do you really think your grandmother will be fooled by this nonsense?' She shook her head. 'I—I can't believe that.'

'Maybe not,' he said. 'But whatever she suspects about my motivation, she can't deny that I've fulfilled her requirements to the letter. And all you have to do, my sweet, is behave, in public, like a girl who's been swept off her feet, and hasn't touched earth since.'

'I see.' She swallowed. 'May I ask, in turn, how you plan to behave? In public?'

He said slowly, 'Like a man who, against all expectation,

and to his own astonishment, has finally met the only woman in the world for him. And is totally bewildered by his undeserved good fortune.'

'Tricky,' she said, 'for someone who clearly believes he's merited all the good things in life.'

He said gently, 'If I ever believed that, Louise, then meeting you would soon have made me think again.'

He got to his feet. Stretched lazily, making her disturbingly conscious of the strength of bone and play of muscle beneath those few yards of silk. Raked back the tawny hair with a careless hand as he strolled to the door.

The Lion King, she thought nervously, *on the prowl.*

In the doorway, he paused and looked back at her. 'While I'm getting dressed, decide how you'd like to spend the day,' he told her casually. 'I'm at your service.'

'Oh, but…' She paused, swallowing. 'There's really no need for you to bother. I—I'll be fine on my own.'

'I don't doubt it,' he said courteously. 'But this is all part of the familiarisation process I mentioned. Persuading you to loosen up.'

She met his gaze. 'Aren't you afraid that familiarity may breed contempt, Mr Fabian?'

'The cobra strikes again.' His mouth smiled but his eyes were hard. 'And the name is Alex—remember. Keep saying it over and over and you'll soon get the hang of it. Just as you'll have to steel yourself to enduring my company for the rest of the day.'

'It seems I have little choice,' she said stiffly. Adding, 'For the rest of the day.'

'Good,' he said mockingly. 'You're learning.' He paused. 'I've arranged to take some time off in the week to spend with you too.'

Louise's eyes widened in dismay. 'Is that strictly necessary?'

'Your enthusiasm flatters me,' he said. 'But there are arrangements to be made. Also, as I've already mentioned, I plan to take you shopping. For one thing, I'd prefer my bride to wear something other than jeans at our wedding,' he added, his eyes flickering over her.

She flushed stormily. 'I'm perfectly capable of choosing something appropriate. I don't need—supervision.'

'No,' he said. 'But you need a trousseau, and I thought some guidance might be helpful.'

'Of course,' she said. 'I'm sure you're an expert on women's clothing.'

'I tend to confine my interest to how easy it is to remove,' he said silkily, and unforgivably. 'But my PA Andie Crane has a more than working knowledge of Bond Street and designer shops and she'd love to show you around. I'll confine myself to buying the ring—if you can spare me the time.'

'Bond Street?' Louise echoed, her face flushed, her mind flinching from the wedding ring and its connotations, among other things. 'You can't be serious. It's ridiculous to spend that kind of money on a—a temporary arrangement.'

'You're going to be my wife,' he said. 'And, for the duration, you will dress accordingly. No chain-store gear, or stuff from a trunk in the attic. Primarily, Andie will help you find a dress for my grandmother's party, and something to wear when you're invited for lunch at the bank.'

'You think I will be?'

'I know it,' he said. 'Because I'm going to be the chairman, and the directors will be forming a line to meet my new bride.'

She said shakily, 'Oh, God—it just gets worse all the time.'

'Don't be scared, darling,' he drawled. 'They won't eat you—unless I give the word. And maybe not even then.'

He added casually, 'Ask Andie to recommend a hairdresser, too, and somewhere to get your nails done.'

Louise stiffened. 'What's wrong with my hair?'

'Nothing,' he said. 'And it would look beautiful spread across my pillow.' He heard her indignant indrawn breath, and grinned. 'But, as that's doomed to remain a private fantasy,' he went on, 'maybe you should have it trimmed a little.'

'Certainly,' she said icily. 'Perhaps I could have a nose job too. Or a breast enlargement. Complete the transformation.'

Alex looked her up and down again, more slowly, his eyes lingering quite deliberately on the rounded curves revealed by the cling of her sweater.

'No,' he said gently. 'No other enhancement is required, believe me.'

Well, I walked into that one, Louise thought, the realisation failing to improve her temper by one iota. I'll have to learn to think before I speak. Or not speak at all...

She mastered herself. Made herself look back at him coolly. She said, 'I'm not a total country mouse. I have been in London before, and I don't need a minder, or a personal shopper. You won't have any reason to feel ashamed of me, whatever the occasion.'

'As you wish,' Alex said after a pause. 'Then let's return to the subject of how we should spend today. I thought of a walk in the park followed by lunch by the river, but I'm open to counter-suggestions.'

'Good,' she said. 'Because you don't need to lead me around the place either. I'm not a visiting tourist.'

'No,' he said softly, 'you're my future wife, and as I've explained I'm simply trying to create a slightly more relaxed situation for us to get to know each other better.'

He paused, leaning against the door frame, his smile thin and suddenly dangerous, setting off alarm signals in her own awareness.

'But we don't have to go out,' he went on cordially. 'We can stay here and—further our acquaintance just as well. A quiet day at home might be just what we need, because who knows where it might lead?' He registered her sudden tension, her widening eyes and lips parting in shock, and his smile widened sardonically. 'And it has the added bonus, of course, that I don't even need to get dressed,' he added gently.

There was a silence that seemed to stretch out, screaming, into infinity.

Then Louise said quietly, huskily, 'On second thoughts, maybe I'd rather go out after all.'

'You have wisdom beyond your years,' Alex said silkily. 'And I shall just have to control my disappointment.'

'I'm sorry.' Her eyes and voice were stony. 'But I'm sure you won't lack for consolation.'

'Well,' he said, 'there's a lot of it about. I won't be lonely.' He paused. 'But you, my sweet, might be. Have you thought of that?'

'No,' she said, with great clarity. 'Because my consolation will be the thought of all the money you're going to pay me.' She took a quick breath. 'And the exquisite certainty that I'll never have to see you again.'

For a brief moment his eyes narrowed, and she thought her words might just have got under his guard.

But the next second he was grinning at her, apparently unmoved. 'In that case,' he told her, 'I'd better make the most of you, darling, while you're around.'

And left her staring after him, her arms wrapped round her body in sudden, uneasy defensiveness. Knowing that it was her own guard, in fact, that was under the real threat.

She thought, Oh, God, I'm going to have to be careful—so very careful…

CHAPTER SIX

In spite of the misgivings which tormented her, Louise found herself forced to admit that a walk had been exactly what she needed. And, traffic fumes notwithstanding, she could not help responding to the warmth and charm of the sunlit day.

There was a real holiday atmosphere in the park, with live music from the bandstand and people sprawled on the grass, with children playing around them and the air filled with voices and laughter.

And, when Alex held out his hand to her, she obeyed his unspoken imperative, after only a brief hesitation, and yielded her fingers to his light clasp.

He was looking good, she acknowledged reluctantly, in pale chinos and a light blue shirt, open at the throat and its cuffs turned back to show off his tan. She was aware of female glances following him with wistful curiosity as she walked at his side.

They'll be wondering how I managed it, she thought with an inward sigh. My God, if they only knew…

Alex took her to lunch at a floating restaurant on the Thames, and the novelty of that, with the sun dancing on the water around them, and the sights and sounds of the great river absorbed her attention satisfactorily until the waiter brought his lamb cutlets and her salade niçoise.

They exchanged a few polite comments about the food, then silence descended again as they ate. Louise found, to her disquiet, that she could not help watching Alex covertly across the table as the meal proceeded. He had classic bone structure, she admitted without pleasure, and incredibly long, gold-tipped eyelashes that might have seemed almost effeminate on someone less confidently male.

In addition, she could remember with terrifying exactness how that coolly humorous mouth had felt when it brushed hers, too, and guessed it was a recollection that would haunt her for a long time.

He had no right to be so attractive, she thought sombrely. Why couldn't he have had an absurd straggly beard, a cast in one eye, or an unsightly mole? Something—anything—that she could have used as a physical focus for her dislike. And which would have made him infinitely easier to resist.

She took a sip of the mineral water she had asked for instead of the wine Alex was drinking, telling herself she needed to keep a clear head.

So far, she thought, her resolve had not been seriously tested. In fact, she found it hard to judge whether or not he'd simply been teasing her with the veiled threats of seduction that she'd found so disturbing.

Which in turn led her to question what might or might not have happened if she'd decided to call his bluff, and spend the day at the flat instead. Recalling, as she did, his comment about seeing her hair spread across his pillow...

And permitting herself to wonder, just for a brief moment, what it would have been like to find herself in his bed, his robe discarded, and Alex intent on his pleasure. And hers.

She thought of his voice, whispering. The late-afternoon sun glinting through drawn curtains onto smooth brown skin. Her own pale by contrast. His weight against her. On her...

'Is it too warm in here?'

She looked up with a guilty start at the sound of Alex's voice, to find him observing her, brows raised quizzically.

'No.' She took another swift gulp of water. 'Everything's—fine. Why do you ask?'

'Because you look rather flushed.' He drank some of his wine, the green eyes speculative. 'What are you thinking about?'

She shrugged, trying to appear insouciant. 'Just that I'm going to need something to do,' she improvised hastily. 'After all, the occasional lunch or party won't fill the time available. And shopping till I drop has never held any attraction for me.'

His brows drew together. 'What are you saying? That you plan to get a job?'

'Would you object?' The forbidden images were beginning to fade. Her breathing to steady.

His frown deepened. 'I do not expect my wife to work,' he said brusquely.

'Then how am I supposed to spend my day?' Louise spread her hands, glad to find they weren't shaking. 'I have no home to run—even the cooking and laundry is done for you. I have no friends here. I can't sit staring at four walls from breakfast to bedtime. I'll get cabin fever.

'Or go mad,' she added. 'They don't let you out of a padded cell to visit the Taj Mahal.'

He didn't smile. 'A lot of people get involved in charity work.'

Louise bit her lip. 'I don't think I'm ready for that yet.' She paused. 'It occurred to me that there might be an opportunity for me at Trentham Osborne.'

'There's certainly a vacancy,' he agreed sardonically. 'I'm not sure you're the right person to fill it.'

'How difficult can it be?' She stopped herself just in time from saying 'Ellie's not that bright', realising that it would almost certainly be interpreted as pure spite, instead of a family truth, always understood but never spoken aloud.

'I wasn't referring to your undoubted abilities,' Alex played with the stem of his glass, 'but the advisability of stepping into your sister's shoes.'

'Why not?' she said harshly. 'She did it to me first.'

'Precisely.' He reached across the table and took her hand, stroking, she realised with shock, the hollow of her palm with his fingertips. Making her catch her breath. Prompting a corresponding curl of sensation to uncoil slowly in the pit of her stomach.

Oh, no, she thought, appalled. This isn't fair. I'm still in recovery.

He said softly, 'Take my advice, darling. Don't do this. Let it go.'

She said hoarsely, 'I can't just—forget…'

'Can't you?' His eyes met hers, smiled into them. 'Why not—try?'

'For one thing it's too soon.' She bit her lip. 'May—may I have my hand back, please?'

'Not yet,' he said. 'But don't worry. I'm not trying to turn you on—even if I believed for one moment that I could. I do have a good reason for this, which I can explain, but not right now.'

'Let me guess,' she said. 'You've seen someone you know. And this is your less than subtle way of letting them know we're an item.'

'If you like.'

'I don't,' she said shortly. 'Wouldn't a simple introduction be better than this—charade?'

'I said it was someone I knew,' he told her. 'I did not mention we were friends.'

He raised her hand to his smiling mouth, his lips tracing the faint blue veins.

His eyes caressed her, openly stripping away the concealing sweater, and the lacy fragment beneath it, making desire an invasion. Sending it running like fire through her blood.

Louise could feel her nipples lift and harden. Instinctively. Involuntarily.

She felt confused suddenly, almost light-headed. Because he was good at this. Oh, God, pretence or not, he was good, and she was no longer in control of her responses.

How—with such little effort—could he make her believe…anything? she asked herself in bewilderment bordering on distress. And, even more dangerously, how could he make her dream?

The arrival of the waiter to remove their empty plates and offer the dessert menu was an intrusion—a shock to her senses.

She felt outraged, as if this polite man, who was only doing his job, had seen her naked. And yet all that had really happened, she thought, was that Alex had released her hand. So really, she ought to be grateful for the interruption.

She heard herself ordering a white peach parfait. Not that she was still hungry, but she needed something to say and do. And asking for food was the simplest option. It restored normality.

'Have some chocolate mousse.' Alex was proffering some on his spoon, and she made herself lean forward and smile and accept it, her still raw senses wincing at the implied intimacy.

'Aren't you going to give me some of your?' he asked.

'Feeding each other with pudding,' she muttered as she complied. 'I can't believe I'm doing this.'

'It's the kind of absurdity lovers indulge in,' he said quietly. 'And you do it very well. Thank you.'

They lingered over coffee and brandy, and when Alex suggested taking a cab back to the flat, Louise demurred.

'I need to walk again,' she said brightly. 'Work off some of those calories.'

'Oh, God,' he said. 'Promise me you're not obsessed with some non-existent weight problem.'

Her smile was unforced. 'I swear I'm not. It just seems a pity to be indoors on such a lovely day,' she added quickly.

'That's one viewpoint,' he said, his glance enigmatic. 'There are others.'

It seemed safer not to pursue that. 'Has your non-friend gone?' she asked instead as they went ashore.

He nodded. 'Some time ago.'

'So you can tell me who it was.'

His mouth tightened. 'It was a journalist,' he said, 'from a particularly sleazy tabloid newspaper. It's not the first time I've been aware of his presence.'

'But why should someone like that be interested in you?' she began, then paused abruptly. 'Or is it your choice of female companion?'

'Clever girl,' he approved sardonically. 'Go to the top of the class.'

She was astonished at the stab of sheer pain that assailed

her. Astonished and ashamed, because she had no right to be feeling like that about anyone when her tears for David were scarcely dry.

And particularly not about Alex.

I despise myself, she thought, wincing.

She braced herself to speak normally as they began to stroll along the Embankment. 'But how did he know where to find you?'

'It's recognised as one of my haunts,' Alex said, shrugging. 'I imagine one of the staff tipped him off.'

'Does it happen often?'

'I'm hoping it soon won't happen at all,' he said drily. 'Once I'm happily married, the gutter Press will cease to trouble about my activities. Or that's the plan, anyway.'

Louise gave a small, wintry smile. 'I didn't realise how useful I was going to be.'

But, of course, he was using her, she told herself as she walked at his side. That was precisely what she'd agreed to.

But there were limits. And she could not afford to let him amuse himself with her with a casual seduction.

It did not help that Alex Fabian was the most physically desirable man she'd ever encountered in her admittedly limited experience. But that was no excuse for her total overreaction just now.

The greatest risk she faced was not Alex's attraction, she thought unhappily, but her own weakness, and she would have to find some way of dealing with it.

Because she needed to emerge from this situation with her pride intact, not as just another notch on his already over-crowded bedpost, she reminded herself tautly.

She was recalled from her troubling thoughts to the equally tricky present by Alex, who came to a sudden halt, muttering a soft but pungent curse under his breath.

'What is it?' Puzzled, Louise turned to look up at him, and saw his mouth twist ruefully.

'Just—this,' he said, and took her by the shoulders, pulling her into his arms, any protest she might have made immediately crushed under the pressure of his lips.

For a moment she was stunned, frozen in disbelief, unable to think—barely able to breathe.

If he'd been brutal she could have fought back, but the searching mouth was gentle as it moved on hers, caressing the soft, trembling contours with slow, enticing patience.

So that, at last, it seemed natural—inevitable—that her lips should part in obedience to his insistence.

The noise of the traffic shrank to a distant murmur. If people turned to look at them, and smile, Louise was oblivious to their stares. The sunlight dazzled her eyes, and permeated her entire body with its golden warmth. Or was it simply the heat of his body, closer to hers than it had ever been?

One hand lifted to stroke her cheek, the line of her jaw, then twined in the soft coils of her hair, making dissent impossible. The other moved down her spine to the small of her back, propelling her forward, their bodies grinding together as if the layers of clothing between them did not exist. His kiss deepened passionately, and she felt the hot, sweet invasion of his tongue exploring the moist inner recesses of her mouth.

She gasped silently, her body arching involuntarily, intimately against his, her hands sliding up to hold his shoulders as the real world began to spin slowly out of control. As she gave way at last to her clamouring instincts and offered her first unguarded response to the demands of his mouth.

And then, as suddenly and shockingly as it had begun, the kiss ended. Not only that, but Alex was also putting her gently but firmly away from him and stepping back, the green eyes narrowed, his expression dispassionate—almost cool. And, she realised with bewilderment and pain, seemingly unmoved by what had just taken place.

When he spoke, there was even faint amusement in his voice. 'Well, he's persistent. I'll give him that.'

Louise found she was taking a pace backwards too, grateful for the support of the stone parapet behind her because her legs were shaking under her.

She said, 'I don't understand. What—who are you talking about?'

'Ed Godwin,' he said. 'The journalist I mentioned. He was following us. Clearly our holding hands over the lunch table didn't convince him that my intentions were serious.'

Hurt twisted like a knife in the pit of her stomach. Dear God, she could still taste him—still bore the imprint of his touch on her body. And it was all pretence. The tenderness she'd sensed—the passion—all a sham. And herself only a fraction away from making an abject fool of herself.

Somehow she snatched at the fragments of her control, her self-respect, and lifted her chin.

She said quietly, 'Then I'm sure your recent performance will have put all his doubts to rest.'

'I certainly hope so,' he said. 'And, if so, he could be useful, keeping the rest of the vultures at bay.'

'You think there'll be more?' She managed to sound politely interested, no more.

He shrugged. 'For a while—until they accept the fact that I'm a married man, and of no further interest to them. That I plan to feature on the financial pages from now on, instead of in the gossip columns.'

'Until our divorce, anyway,' she pointed out.

'Perhaps,' he said. 'But I'll deal with that when I have to.'

'So, what happened to our stalker?'

'He hailed a black cab, and pushed off.'

And you, she thought, couldn't wait to push me away...

She said, 'Then I suggest we do the same. I think I've had enough fresh air for one day.'

'As you wish,' Alex said equably. He paused. 'Louise, I'm sorry if I took you by surprise just now, but I could hardly warn you in advance.'

'Please,' she said, 'you don't have to apologise—or explain.'

'Naturally I'm concerned,' he said. He hesitated again. 'I hope you didn't find my ardour—a little excessive.'

'A little, maybe.' She even managed a smile as cool as his

own. 'But I can hardly complain. After all, that's what you're paying me for. Isn't it?'

And she turned and walked away from him, head high, and her shaking hands thrust safely out of sight in her pockets, leaving him staring after her.

Two weeks later they were married in a ceremony so brief and formal that Louise could almost have thought it a fleeting dream, but for the sudden presence of Alex's wedding ring on her hand.

She supposed there would come a time when its golden gleam would not seem so alien, but, in a way, it was the least of her problems.

After the incident on the Embankment, she had decided that her only recourse was to treat the whole situation as a game. And a game with strict rules from which there could not be the slightest deviation.

And it seemed that Alex must have had similar thoughts during that silent taxi ride back to the flat, because ever since they had behaved with almost rigorous civility on the occasions when they were together, walking round each other as if they were treading on eggshells.

To her surprise, he had kept his word about the written contract she'd demanded.

'Here.' He'd tossed it into her lap. 'I hope this is the reassurance you wanted about my good intentions.'

Louise had read it, her eyes widening. 'Generous isn't the word,' she had said when she'd caught her breath. 'I feel as if I've won the lottery.'

'I'm glad you're pleased,' he'd said politely. 'However, if you're looking for the non-molestation clause, forget it. My lawyer's eyes were popping out of his head as it was. So I'm afraid you'll just have to take my word that I won't touch you—or not without your express invitation, anyway.'

She had stared down at the typed words until they blurred. 'Then I'll just have to rely on that.'

But so far she had no real complaints. She had to admit that

Alex had made things easier by spending a minimum of time at the flat, and she was managing to accept his appearances as well as his prolonged and unexplained absences with apparent equanimity.

She was slowly becoming accustomed to her new environment, too. The weather had been mainly fine and warm, encouraging her to spend a lot of time in the roof garden. She even sunbathed sometimes in the black bikini she'd bought for that very reason. She could even indulge her passion for reading as never before, and she'd also purchased a portable CD player so that she could listen to music and drama on disc while she relaxed.

It was, she thought, almost a life. And if her heart leapt painfully when she heard his key in the lock, then that was a secret she kept well-hidden, desperately ashamed of her own weakness.

Besides, if she seemed awkward or withdrawn at any time, she could always imply she was still heartbroken over David and Ellie. And only she would know it was a lie.

However, she supposed, they would both have to lower their guard a little for his grandmother's birthday party—the next ordeal to be endured—if she did not count the forthcoming wedding celebration at the Savoy.

'It was not my idea,' Alex had told her flatly the night before. 'My father insisted.'

Louise bit her lip. She had met George Fabian only once, a difficult rather stilted encounter at the Ritz. He had concealed his astonishment at his son's choice of wife with smiling good manners, but Louise was tautly aware that he knew the exact reason for this amazing mismatch. Knew it—and disapproved.

'Well,' she'd said, 'I'm sure he means to be—kind. And you did ask him to be one of our witnesses.'

'Yes,' he'd said. 'I thought one of us at least should have a blood relative present.'

Louise flushed. Her visit to Trentham Osborne to inform her father that the wedding date had been set was not a treasured memory. But neither was reporting on it later to a cynical Alex.

'Belated guilty conscience, darling?' he'd inquired pleasantly, after she'd stumbled through her explanation that a long-planned trip to the States would prevent her father from attending their marriage. 'Could he be feeling bad about selling you to me?'

'No,' she denied defensively. 'He has all these meetings set up that he can't postpone.' She forbore to add that she had no chance of any kind of job with the family firm, her father having stared at her in disbelief before impatiently brushing her tentative enquiry aside. She did not want to hear Alex say that he'd told her so.

She paused. 'And Marian is still down at the cottage, waiting to hear from Ellie. So that's that.' *And in London, her father was doing exactly the same thing, and she knew it.* She tried to smile. 'Anyway, I'm glad that you invited Andie instead. I—I like her.'

She had not expected to do so. In fact, she'd been angry when Alex had ignored her protests, and insisted on his PA acting as her guide and mentor round the London fashion houses.

But Andie Crane had proved to be a slim blonde, whose high-powered chic had been set off by her merry face and insouciant manner, and who had clearly no intention of forcing her own tastes or opinions on her boss's bride.

She herself had been married for less than a year, she'd confided, and had found the run-up to her own wedding positively nerve-racking. 'And I had months to spend on the planning,' she said, laughing. 'Whereas you've had days rather than weeks. Although maybe it's better that way,' she added more thoughtfully. 'Less time for second thoughts.'

Second, third, fourth and fifth, Louise thought wearily. With more to come.

She said quietly, 'I don't think Alex would allow them, anyway.'

Andie's eyes twinkled. 'Probably not.'

She must have been burning to know the story behind this

unholy dash into matrimony, but was far too discreet to ask questions or attempt to invade Louise's confidence.

And the hairdresser she recommended was a revelation, expertly layering Louise's unruly dark curls into an altogether sleeker and more manageable style that also gave her, she felt, a much needed edge of sophistication.

While shopping, she soon discovered, could be fun with a knowledgeable companion—and, admittedly, when money, too, was no object.

Andie's idea of a trousseau ranged from outfits for every conceivable occasion down to the prettiest, sexiest lingerie that Louise had ever possessed. Gossamer stuff, primarily designed to appeal to male senses, she realised, biting her lip. And totally wasted on her.

A visit to a beauty salon resulted in a make-up lesson, which she enjoyed, and a pastel leather case equipped with co-ordinated replacements for her own hotchpotch of cosmetics, which Andie advised her to ditch.

The pale pink sheath Louise wore for the much dreaded lunch at Perrins Bank had been bought on Andie's advice, too.

'Men love pink, especially the older ones,' she said. 'You'll wow them.'

A slight exaggeration, perhaps, Louise thought, but the lunch had went better than she could have hoped, her obvious shyness doing her no disservice at all.

'Well done,' was Alex's laconic comment when it was over, and she was disconcerted to find herself beaming as if she'd received some accolade.

Even the search for a wedding dress that was not too overtly bridal proved simplicity itself in the end. A small boutique in Knightsbridge produced a slender shift in ivory silk, high-necked and sleeveless, topped with a matching hip-length jacket, narrowly edged in gold, which floated as she moved. Plain kid court shoes and a tiny bag on a long gold chain completed the ensemble.

It was a far cry from the billowing white gown and veil she'd always envisaged, but then nothing about this marriage was like anything she'd ever contemplated—not even in her wildest nightmares.

And now it was done. She'd made her promises in a small, calm voice, and become Mrs Alex Fabian, currently on her way to lunch at the Savoy in the chauffeur-driven car which had also, somehow, become part of her everyday life. Proof, if proof were needed, that Alex was a man who liked his own way, and expected to get it—even in minor matters.

He had kept his word about taking her to buy the wedding ring.

They'd gone to a discreetly exclusive jewellers, where they were shown into a private panelled room, offered a glass of excellent sherry, and where Louise's finger was ceremoniously measured.

Tray after velvet-covered tray was then brought out for their inspection. So many shades of gold—Alex having decisively rejected platinum—in so many styles. Wide or narrow, plain or chased, no two rings seemed the same.

Louise had expected that the whole thing would only take a few minutes. That Alex, conscious that it was only a temporary measure, would make a swift selection, pretty much at random.

She was embarrassed too by the kindly smiles of the middle-aged jeweller, who so obviously believed they were happy lovers choosing a ring that would last their entire lives long.

I'm a fraud, she wanted to tell him. And we might as well use a brass curtain ring.

But she said nothing, and when Alex picked out a plain, elegant ring in a medium width, she smiled as he slipped it onto her other hand, and murmured truthfully that it was beautiful.

Now, seated beside him in the car, she stared down at the flowers she was holding—tiny cream and gold roses, their petals just unfurling, and tried not to think about the inevitabilities of the future. About the strain of maintaining the pretence, the topics of conversation that, for safety's sake, remained strictly taboo. And, of course, the strict avoidance of all physical contact when they were alone. So that they seemed like two people trapped in separate vacuums. Isolated. Unreachable.

But that was the way she wanted it, she reminded herself, and the way it had to be. Because anything else would be unthinkable.

Alex had kissed her when they were pronounced man and wife, because it was expected of him. A swift, formal brush of his lips on hers that meant nothing, and would cause no restless, unhappy dreams. Or so she could only hope, she told herself as the car drew up in front of the famous Savoy façade.

George Fabian had reserved a table overlooking the river, where champagne was waiting, expertly iced. And, although she could not decide whether it was the wine, or the fact that she was finally married—committed, with no way back—that was the cause, she found herself able to relax a little and almost enjoy herself as her health was drunk.

The food was delicious too, with tiny asparagus tartlets being followed by poussins in a wine sauce, with straw potatoes and tender French beans. A rich confection of raspberries whisked into thick and alcoholic cream ended the meal.

Louise would have lingered over the coffee and petits fours, but to her surprise George Fabian was glancing at his watch and murmuring about appointments, and Andie, in a blue linen dress that matched her eyes, was saying briskly that she too needed to get back to Perrins.

Oh, God, Louise thought, staring at the tablecloth as if it fascinated her. They're being tactful. Even his father, who knows precisely why we went through that ceremony this morning, thinks that Alex will want to be alone with me. That, now I'm his wife, he has a right to take full advantage of the circumstances, and won't hesitate to do so.

She groaned inwardly, realising that Andie, who worked for him, and presumably knew his reputation, would imagine her as a more than willing bride, eager to respond to his expertise as a lover.

She made herself look up, swallowing, and found Alex

watching her, the green eyes hooded and enigmatic, and her heart lurched in a kind of panic mingled with excitement.

'It's such a pity that your honeymoon has to be postponed,' Andie sympathised quietly as they all made their way to the main entrance. 'But there's so much going on at Perrins now that Alex has definitely been confirmed as the next chairman. He really can't afford to take any time off just now.'

Louise bit her lip. 'It's—not a problem. Really.'

'No?' Andie's expression was faintly puzzled. 'Well, I expect Alex will choose somewhere extra-glamorous and romantic to make up for it,' she added cheerfully. 'When the time comes.' She gave Louise a swift hug. 'Enjoy the rest of your day,' she added with a wicked grin.

Louise stood beside Alex, waving goodbye as the cabs containing George Fabian and Andie went off in their different directions, and smiling so determinedly that it hurt.

Alone at last. The words came into her mind, along with Andie's mischievous, knowing smile, and would not go away. She felt a faint shiver—half dread, half longing—run along her nerve-endings.

As she turned away Alex's hand closed on her arm, and she glanced at him, her eyes blank with sudden alarm.

'Don't worry,' he said softly. 'I don't think the Savoy rents rooms by the afternoon.' He paused. 'Although I could always ask.'

She hated herself for blushing. She said coldly, 'Please don't be absurd.'

'It's a fairly absurd situation,' he returned shortly. He paused. 'I have a meeting to go to in the City. Have you any plans for the rest of the afternoon? May I drop you somewhere?'

She shook her head slowly. Suddenly, she felt that she was the absurd one here, all dressed up with, patently, nowhere to go. And no one to go with.

She said, 'You mean you're going back to work?'

'You have some objection?'

'None,' she said swiftly. 'Only Andie didn't mention it.'

'Andie doesn't know,' Alex said shortly. 'I arranged this meeting yesterday, after she'd left for the day.'

It was her wedding day, and she was being left totally to her own devices. And he hadn't even said she looked nice, she thought childishly. Not even when she'd stood beside him in front of the registrar. Just one brief, unsmiling glance as he took her hand.

She sighed inwardly, soundlessly. 'I think I'll go back to the flat.'

'As you wish.' He signalled and the car drew up in front of them.

He was clearly impatient to be off. To be rid of her, and that hurt. Yet another absurdity, she thought.

She said carefully, as they emerged into the Strand, 'Alex— is there anything wrong? Have I—done something?'

'No, my sweet.' His mouth twisted. 'Your behaviour has been faultless throughout.'

'Then what is it?' She tried to smile. 'If you've decided you don't want to be a married man, after all, you've left it rather late.'

'But that's exactly it,' he said, and she could hear the faint throb of anger under his even tone. 'You see, I discovered there in the registry office that marriage doesn't suit me, Louise. It doesn't suit me at all. Yet here I am, the condemned man hearing the doors of the prison cage slam behind him—and knowing that he's trapped.'

Pain tore through her. She managed, just in time, to suppress a little, shocked gasp.

She said stonily, 'Then it's a trap entirely of your own making. I just hope you think your precious inheritance is worth it.'

'At the moment I have my doubts,' he returned bleakly.

They didn't exchange another word until they arrived outside the block of flats.

'Do you want me to come in with you?' He was frowning faintly, not looking at her, as if his mind had already leapt ahead to his City appointment.

'No,' she said, 'thank you. Let's just get on with the rest of our lives—shall we? And don't look so furious,' she added, striving for lightness. 'Play your cards right, and you might get time off for good behaviour.'

She slammed the door of the car, and stalked across the pavement to the massive glass doors which the commissionaire was holding open for her, and went inside.

She was shaking with anger as she rode up in the lift. She was helping him, and he couldn't even be bothered to make the day special for her.

He thought he was in prison? she thought, seething, as she let herself into the flat. Well, this was her cage too. It was luxurious—gold-plated even—but the bars were there just the same. And she was in solitary confinement.

But in her case, this was a cage she did not want to leave—ever...

She came to a stunned halt halfway across the living room, standing white-faced and motionless, staring into space, as she considered the implications of this unwanted revelation.

As she recognised, with a silent scream of anguish, that—somehow and unbelievably—she had fallen in love with Alex. No—more than that. That she loved him, and that was why he filled her thoughts by day, and haunted her dreams in the long, lonely nights.

Alex, she thought, shivering, who cared nothing for her. Who was already resenting his lost freedom, and, indeed, planning to discard her at the earliest opportunity.

He doesn't want me, she reminded herself with swift, searing desolation. He never did, and he never will. And I have the written contract to prove it.

And—God help me—there isn't a thing I can do about it.

CHAPTER SEVEN

SHE sat for a long time in the corner of the sofa, twisting the wedding band on her finger, while the slow, scalding tears trickled down her face and dripped off the end of her nose.

She was being ridiculous, and she knew it, but all other choices had been removed in the light of her recent self-revelation.

She might argue with herself that it wasn't love but simply physical attraction, triggered by that kiss, and that, left untended, it would wither and die of its own accord. But a female instinct she'd never known she possessed told her otherwise.

Suggested that she'd actually been fighting her awareness of him from day one. That there'd been a moment when that awareness had transmuted into an aching need. When he'd become part of the essence of her day, and to see him, and hear his voice brought their own meagre satisfaction. Because that might be all that she would ever have of him.

After all, Alex had married her purely for convenience. Because he needed a token wife as a weapon in this private battle he was waging with his grandmother. It was a financial transaction, as he'd made clear. A solution to their mutual problems. A business deal, offered and accepted without emotion, or so she'd convinced herself.

Well, she'd been half right. Because the only emotion on his side was clearly regret. He'd married her in haste, and repented instantly.

He'd chosen her in the first place because she was not attractive to him, and therefore easily expendable when her usefulness to him was at an end.

His attempts to seduce her had never been wholly serious, she reminded herself painfully. Just another conditioned reflex from a man who was accustomed to having a girl in his bed, and because she was there—in his life, on the premises. A little enjoyable lust without commitment.

Most of it had simply been sexual teasing anyway, used solely to catch her off-balance—to flurry her into doing precisely what he wanted. And it had worked, she admitted ruefully, because she'd never been brave enough to call his bluff, and he knew it.

But even if he'd been genuinely tempted to amuse himself with her for a night or two, instinct would probably have warned him that she wasn't the type for casual sex. That her lack of experience would soon pall. And that she might not want to 'kiss and part' when it was over.

That was why he chose me, she thought wretchedly. Because my demands were going to be financial, not emotional, and he could handle that. Because I wouldn't make a nuisance of myself.

Looking back, she could see that perhaps her unguarded, ardent response to his kiss had set alarm bells ringing. Hinted that maybe she wasn't as indifferent as she pretended. And this was why he'd avoided her so studiously ever since.

Louise drew a long, trembling sigh. She could hardly believe what was happening to her. What she was allowing to happen. Or what she was thinking. Because, on the face of it, Alex Fabian was the last man in the world she should ever want, and she knew it.

Her ideal man had always been someone quiet, rugged and totally dependable. Someone who was ready to settle down, in some quiet backwater, and be happy.

Someone like David...

That same David, she derided herself bitterly, who'd run off with her stepsister. Well, good thinking, Girl Wonder!

Whereas Alex, who lived his life unashamedly in the fast lane, and who found even the prospect of monogamy boring, was at least honest about it. Too honest at times, she thought, smearing away her tears with her fingers, as she recalled his coldness in the car, his anger at the pit he'd unthinkingly dug for himself, blinded by everything but his obsession with a house.

As the love of her life, he promised to be a complete disaster, she thought, an unwilling smile quivering on her lips.

But love, when it came, wasn't sensible or realistic. Nor did it wait to be invited, as she'd so ruinously discovered. It took possession, mind, soul and body, and stretched you on the rack of your own senses and emotions.

With David, however mistakenly, she'd felt safe. But loving Alex was like falling from the high-wire without a net. The ultimate risk, as he'd once warned her himself.

And, as a result, she could well end up in pieces that would never mend.

If she allowed it to happen…

Because there was no need for him to feel trapped, she told herself. Contract or not, he could afford the best lawyers in the world to free him from this non-marriage which had so quickly turned sour. Surely they could arrange an equally speedy annulment?

But why hadn't he spoken while they were standing in front of the registrar? she wondered. Just 'I can't do this' would have been enough to stop the whole thing in its tracks. It would have been cruel, but kinder in the long term. And better than this terrible limbo where she now found herself.

She got up wearily, and went down the corridor to her bedroom. She paused for a moment, staring at her wan reflection in the long wall mirror. So different from the hopeful girl in the shimmering, floating silk who'd looked back at her that morning. Who, without realising why, had expected—longed for—her bridegroom's approval.

It was one of the conventions that you cried at weddings, she thought, her mouth twisting ruefully, but not usually your own.

In fact, her primary instinct, fired by the blind rush of anger that had carried her up in the lift, had been to strip off her wedding dress and hack it to pieces with her nail scissors.

Obliterate it, just as the marriage itself would eventually be erased.

Now she took it off and put it carefully on a hanger, placing it at the back of one of the fitted wardrobes where it would be lost among all the other clothes.

It was so lovely, but it hadn't changed a thing, she thought, although that was hardly the dress's fault. When she could bear to look at it again, she'd donate it to a charity shop.

She rescued her bouquet from the living room floor where she'd dropped it, gently unwiring the roses and placing them in a vase beside her bed. Because Alex had bought them for her. Stupid, she knew. Pathetic, but she couldn't help herself.

Then she ran a bath scented with geranium oil, and sank down into it, emptying her mind, and letting the warm water do its healing, washing away the marks of her tears.

Recriminations were useless, she thought as she padded back into her room, wrapped in an enormous, fluffy bath sheet. After all, she knew the conditions. She'd walked into this situation with her eyes wide open, and now she had to deal with the consequences.

And, whatever else happened, Alex must never know that she loved him. She was heading for heartbreak as it was, so total humiliation might just be more than she could bear, she thought with irony.

Therefore, when Alex returned, all traces of the unwanted bride would have been removed, and cool practical Louise would be in place again, neutral in her jeans and T-shirt. The girl who made no demands, and invaded no space. Calm and casually friendly.

And if he'd decided in the meantime that he still wanted to go on with this charade, and needed her to play the role he had assigned to her, then she would adhere strictly to the script from now on. In particular, the lines for his grandmother's party, which would take place next weekend.

Louise winced. That would prove an overwhelming test for their fragile bargain, she thought apprehensively. And if Alex was still in resentful mourning for his lost bachelor status then they wouldn't deceive a child of three. This was just one of the points she needed to raise with him when he returned.

When he returned...

Louise said the words aloud, and sighed, knowing that she had never felt so entirely alone in the whole of her life.

The hours dragged slowly past. At some point in the evening Louise went into the kitchen and cooked the seafood risotto she'd planned originally as a celebration dinner, in the forlorn hope that Alex would be there to share it with her.

And how sad is that? she asked herself impatiently, pouring herself a glass of the crisp white wine she'd chosen to accompany the meal.

When they'd first met, he'd praised her cooking. He'd even suggested she was good enough to be a professional. Yet, since she'd been living with him, the only thing she'd been allowed to prepare was coffee.

But, as the doors of Trentham Osborne were closed to her, she could always try to get a job in catering—providing corporate lunches, perhaps, like the efficient, smiling girls in the smart blue uniforms who'd served the meal at Perrins that day.

It was something to consider anyway. Because she couldn't spend her life cooped up in the lap of luxury. For one thing, it would give her too much time to think.

She ate her risotto with due appreciation, glad that she did not appear to be losing her touch. She allowed herself two glasses of wine only with her meal, because she needed to keep a clear head, as never before. There were matters she needed to settle with Alex, and the sooner the better. Preferably tonight.

Dishes washed, and the kitchen tidied, she went back into the living room and watched some television, only half concentrating on the images in front of her, more concerned about what she would say to Alex—when he returned. And how she was going to be able to hide her true feelings for him.

It was only when her eyelids drooped and she began to doze that she realised how late it was. That midnight had come and gone, and there was still no sign of him. Surely he'd be back soon, she thought, trying to soothe her own anxiety.

But when another hour had passed she finally admitted defeat, and went to bed.

But she couldn't rest. Although she was tired, she was still listening for some sound that would tell her that Alex had come home at last.

And she could never be sure when she made herself face the fact that he probably hadn't been whisked to hospital with a mystery virus, or knocked down by a bus.

No, the truth was undoubtedly far simpler, she thought, her heart thudding painfully against her rib cage. Because she had to accept that Alex was almost certainly celebrating the first night of his marriage in the arms of some other woman.

A little moan rose to her lips, and she turned over, burying her face in the pillow to muffle the sound and blot out the troubling—the unbearable—images invading her mind.

And when she eventually fell asleep she dreamed she was running through a wild and rocky world, endlessly calling his name, but receiving no reply.

She awoke the next morning feeling jaded, a faint, nagging ache lodged above her eyebrows.

I need coffee, she told herself, wearily reaching for her dressing gown.

On her way to the kitchen, she paused by Alex's bedroom. The door was open, and one glance showed the wide bed still unused and pristine. He had truly been gone all night, she thought, her heart dropping like a stone.

She filled the cafetière, and carried it into the living room. She'd filled her beaker, and taken her first cautious sip, when she heard the front door open and close. She stood very still, the colour draining from her face, and a moment later Alex appeared.

His tie was missing, his waistcoat unbuttoned and his shirt open at the neck, but he was still in the same clothes he'd worn for the wedding. His eyes were bloodshot, and there was a shadow of stubble on his chin.

He looked, she thought, as if he had been drinking, too.

She said quietly, 'You're home.'

'Is that how you think of this place?' Alex glanced around him, his brows lifted cynically. 'How quaint.'

Louise decided it would be better to ignore that.

She said, 'You—didn't come back last night.'

'Obviously,' he said coolly. 'I thought you'd probably be glad to be spared my presence—it being our wedding night.'

His smile did not reach his eyes as he registered the sudden defensive stiffening of her slim figure.

'Such an evocative phrase, that, don't you think, darling?' he drawled derisively. 'So full of—resonances. Only I really wasn't in the mood to deal with them. Or not in any way that you would have wished for anyway,' he added.

Louise looked down at the floor. She said in a low voice, 'I was—worried. I didn't know where you were.'

'Do you really want the details?' he asked mockingly. 'Of where I spent the night? In what bed?'

Her immediate impulse was to wrap her arms round her body in self-protection. But that would be instant self-betrayal—letting him see that he had the power to hurt her. And she was in agony, even though he'd merely confirmed her own worst suspicions.

Instead, she lifted her chin, facing him again.

She said crisply. 'It's really none of my concern. In future, I'll simply take it for granted that you'll be staying elsewhere.'

His mouth twisted. 'You are gracious beyond my desserts.'

'No,' she said. 'Just indifferent.' She paused. 'So what happens now? Am I supposed to make you a free man again by divorcing you? If that's the plan, I imagine your tabloid friend will have a field-day, and you'll lose any remaining chance of claiming Rosshampton.' She shrugged. 'But it's your choice.'

'How could I possibly want to rid myself of such an understanding wife?' There was a faint jeering note in his voice. 'No, my sweet, we'll let the marriage stand.'

She bit her lip. 'Very well.' She surveyed him stonily. 'You look terrible.'

'Thank you,' he returned courteously. 'But a bath and a shave will soon restore me. And no one is going to be surprised if I look as if I didn't sleep much last night.' His smile glinted. 'Under the circumstances, they'll expect it.'

To her fury, Louise felt her face warm. Worse still, she was aware of the sudden bitterness of tears in her throat.

With a superhuman effort, she kept her voice steady. 'Please help yourself to coffee. You look as if you need it.'

She picked up her beaker and started towards the door, desperate to get to the sanctuary of her room.

As she passed him, Alex put a detaining hand on her arm. 'Louise—listen…'

Coffee splashed onto the floor as she shook him off, her eyes blazing. 'You don't touch me when we're alone, remember?' she said hoarsely. 'Not now, or ever. And in public only when strictly necessary. That's the deal, Alex, and if you break it I will go. I swear it.' She drew a swift, uneven breath, wanting to hurt him in turn. 'Don't you understand? You make me feel—contaminated.'

He was very pale suddenly, his mouth taut. 'And, of course, we can't have that, my little plaster saint.' There was icy bitterness in his voice. 'I just hope you won't get too lonely up there on your self-righteous pedestal.'

She gasped, anger surging up inside her, overwhelming the pain, the bewilderment, and the aching, desperate need. Before she could think, her hand swung back, and the remains of her coffee were sent showering over him.

For a second she stood transfixed, watching his expression change from astonishment and disbelief to something altogether more dangerous. Then she dropped the empty beaker and fled to her room, slamming the door and turning the key in the lock with clumsy fingers.

She leaned against the panels, listening tensely, half expecting him to come after her, but after a moment or two she heard him go into his own room, and close the door.

And later still she heard him leave, presumably for the bank. It was weak and self-indulgent to feel relief, but she did. She sank down to the carpet, her back against the door, her clenched fist pressed to her quivering mouth.

A small sound between a laugh and a sob escaped her. So much for calm, she thought, not to mention casually friendly.

'And welcome to married life,' she whispered, staring dry-eyed and unseeing into space.

The flowers arrived during the afternoon. More roses—deep crimson this time—and carnations and lilies in an exquisite, heady arrangement, filling the room with their scent. The card said simply 'Alex'.

A peace-offering, Louise wondered as she placed them on the coffee table, or a wreath?

Even more surprisingly, he arrived himself not long after six p.m. Louise had been curled up on the sofa, watching the television news, prepared for another solitary evening, if not an action for assault.

As he came in she pressed the mute button on the remote control and got to her feet, eyeing him apprehensively.

But his face was cool, unreadable. 'I see you got the flowers.'

'Yes,' she said. 'I thought they might be wired to a bomb.'

'And I expected to find them splattered all over the pavement.' He propped a shoulder against the door frame, watching her.

'Why did you send them?'

His mouth twisted wryly. 'I felt some gesture was called for. But I'm not into grovelling. And I thought the thing with the coffee wouldn't work so well a second time,' he added, deadpan.

Louise flushed. 'No.' She swallowed. 'I—I don't usually do things like that.'

'You mean like losing your self-control,' he said. 'I've noticed.'

Wiser not to respond to that, she decided.

Instead, she said, 'I hope I didn't ruin your beautiful suit.'

'The dry-cleaners tell me it will live.'

She lifted her chin. 'I'm sorry.'

'Why? I asked for it.' He studied her for a moment. 'I didn't even tell you how lovely you looked yesterday,' he added unexpectedly. 'I was the envy of every man at the Savoy.'

Lovely, she thought, *but not lovely enough…*

'I doubt that very much,' she said. 'But—thank you, anyway. I know how appearances matter,' she added stiltedly.

Alex reached behind him and produced a carrier bag. 'To make further amends, I've brought food. I thought we might have dinner together.'

'Dinner?' Louise echoed, stunned. 'You want me to cook you dinner?'

'I hoped we could make some kind of fresh start.' He shrugged. 'But if you'd prefer not to, I shall understand. It's nothing too outrageous—just a couple of fillet steaks and some salad. I could probably manage that myself.'

In spite of herself, she found her mouth trembling into a smile. 'I bet you didn't go out and buy all that yourself. I bet you sent Andie.'

His own face relaxed too. 'Considering we live as strangers,' he drawled, 'you're getting to know me too damned well.' He paused. 'Do you want me to cook dinner?'

'No,' she said. 'I'll do that, and you can pour the wine. That sounds like a fair division of labour.'

That was friendly and casual enough for anyone, she thought as she went into the kitchen. But calm was nowhere within reach. Her heart was going like a triphammer, and there was an odd trembling in the pit of her stomach.

She had spent a wretched day, trying and failing to dismiss from her mind the unwanted images of Alex with some unknown woman that kept constantly invading her consciousness, and tormenting her. It was, she thought, like mistakenly finding herself at the showing of some erotic movie, and being unable to leave.

Nor was there any guarantee that the woman he'd been with was unknown to her. Because, ever since their brief meeting,

Cindy Crosby's beautiful face and voluptuous figure had never been far away from her mind.

She had realised almost at once that it must be that particular liaison which had attracted the attention of the gutter Press. The Crosbys were news, his political career seriously on the move. Not long ago, there'd even been a full-colour spread about them in one of the gossip magazines, showing them in their Surrey home, the picture of marital devotion, complete with manicured lawns and the obligatory Labradors.

'Lucinda's my rock,' her husband had gushed. 'Always there for me.'

Except, Louise thought cynically, when she was elsewhere, and not alone.

Alex's sudden marriage might have thrown Ed Godwin and his like temporarily off the scent, but one hint that he was still involved with the lovely Cindy would bring them back in full cry, and Louise could only imagine the kind of scandal that would ensue—and its ruinous consequences.

But she had told Alex to his face that she did not care what he did, or where he went, and now, somehow, she had to live up to those brave words, whatever the personal cost. Hide the fact that the vividly sensuous pictures in her imagination were tearing her apart, giving her no peace. Present a façade of indifference when her entire being seemed to be one silent scream of jealous misery. And fear…

She moved round the kitchen like an automaton, trying to put these thoughts from her mind, collecting the ingredients for a salad dressing from the store cupboard she'd begun to build during her shopping expeditions.

'Is there anything I can do?' He appeared beside her so quietly and suddenly that Louise jumped, nearly dropping the mustard on the floor.

'Everything's under control.' She mustered a taut smile. 'Andie's done us proud. There are baby new potatoes to go with the steak, and a tarte au citron for pudding.'

He leaned against the refrigerator. 'May I watch, or will it disturb you?'

Everything about you disturbs me, she thought with sudden, savage longing. Even when you're unshaven, hung-over and exhausted, as you were this morning. Even when I know you've just climbed out of another woman's bed. And I can't help myself.

The way your hair grows back from your forehead disturbs me. The line of your jaw. Your hands. The way you move. How you laugh with your eyes when your mouth stays solemn. Your mouth—oh, God—your mouth most of all...

Aloud, she said, 'Be my guest.'

'Can we talk, or do you want me to keep quiet?'

'Not at all,' she said. She paused. 'Is there anything particular you want to say?' *Or confess?*

'No,' he said, 'I don't think so.'

She summoned a forced smile. 'Then why don't you tell me about Rosshampton?'

'What do you want to know?'

She began to mix the dressing. 'Maybe—why you love it so much.'

He said slowly, 'I suppose because it's always represented comfort, safety—and security.'

'All the things I wanted from David.' She reached for the olive oil.

'True,' he said. 'But bricks and mortar tend to be more reliable.'

She bit her lip. 'Why did you spend so much time there?'

'My parents had a fairly chequered marriage.' His tone was brusque. 'My father was abroad a great deal on business when I was young. Although he loved my mother, he never regarded fidelity as a major issue, which did not endear him to Selina. My mother did, so she decided it was safer to travel with him. Therefore I stayed at home with my grandmother at Rosshampton.'

'That must have been hard on you,' Louise said in a low voice, her mind wincing away from this confirmation that unfaithfulness was a Fabian trait.

'Please don't regard me as a lonely waif.' Alex spoke with

a certain asperity. 'Believe me, I never lacked for a thing, including affection. Even when my mother died, Selina was there for me, like a rock, although she must have been dying inside herself at the loss of her only child.'

'Yes,' she said slowly. 'I—I'm so sorry.'

Alex stared at the floor. 'It was a brain haemorrhage,' he said too evenly. 'She was only ill for a couple of hours. They were in New York, and my father had just come back from the pharmacy with some painkillers for the headache she'd complained of, and she smiled at him and simply—went...'

He shook his head. 'He was very withdrawn for a long time. Eventually, he started going out—meeting up with friends and, of course, seeing women. Everyone said it was only a matter of time before he married again. But they were so wrong. She was the one—the real thing in his life. Everything else was just a trivial diversion. And still is, as far as I know.'

She said quietly, 'Thank you for telling me.'

There was a silence as she rinsed the potatoes, and placed them in the steamer.

'Is that new?' Alex enquired.

'Well, yes,' she admitted. 'I hope you don't mind.'

His brows lifted. 'Do I look as if I mind?'

No, she thought bitterly, the breath catching in her throat. He looked as he always did—tanned, tawny and too damned sexy for his own good...or hers.

She said hurriedly, 'Tell me something about the house itself.'

He shrugged. 'It's just a big country house, surrounded by trees. Said to date from Queen Anne's time, but much added to since. Has a ballroom at the rear and ten bedrooms, not including the Royal Suite.'

'Royal?' Louise turned the salad leaves into a bowl, and added the dressing. 'That sounds very imposing.'

'It's extremely comfortable,' he returned. 'Two bedrooms, with a sitting room in between, plus dressing room and bathroom. Apparently Queen Victoria stayed there once or twice with Prince Albert.'

'Then why two bedrooms?' Louise lit the grill for the steaks. 'I thought she was crazy about Albert—couldn't get enough of him.'

'Perhaps he liked the occasional night off,' Alex suggested blandly. And, heaven help her, he was doing that thing with his mouth and eyes again. 'Whatever, that's where we'll be sleeping. Selina always puts me in there when I stay—which is convenient.' He paused. 'Shall I set the table?'

'All by yourself?' Louise asked dulcetly. 'Or will you ring for someone?'

'You, my sweet,' he said softly, 'are asking for trouble. Less of it.'

When she carried the food to the dining room, she found to her surprise that the dining room looked a picture, the polished table set with linen place-mats, gleaming cutlery and glassware, and lit by tall candles in polished silver holders.

She whistled. 'Isn't this a little OTT?'

'Perhaps,' Alex said. 'But it could be the first and last time we ever do this, so let's go for it.'

She flashed him a too-bright smile. 'You're right. Let's.'

She would never forget this evening as long as she lived, she thought later as she sat across the table from Alex in the candlelight. The food and wine were delectable, but, even better, she found suddenly that they were chatting like old friends. In a strange way, even the occasional silences were companionable.

'Do you realise,' she said, 'that I don't even know when your birthday is?'

'It's not a closely guarded secret.' Alex finished his slice of tarte au citron. 'Try August the fifth.'

'Ah,' she said. 'Leo. I should have known.'

He sighed. 'I see someone's told you my nickname.'

'Does it bother you?'

'Not in the slightest.' He paused. 'Do you like the wine?'

'It's wonderful,' she said. 'I can taste cherries.'

'Well done.' Alex smiled at her. 'Maybe I should take you on a tour of the French wine regions.'

'You forget,' Louise said. 'I already have my future itinerary all mapped out.'

'Yes,' he said, 'I almost did forget. But thanks for reminding me.' He was silent for a moment. 'Would you like brandy with your coffee?'

She shook her head. 'Nothing more for me, thanks. I'll clear away, and then I think I'll have an early night.'

'You're allowed to stay up until midnight, Cinderella.'

Not, she thought, when you're trying to catch up on last night's sleep.

She shrugged. 'All the same...'

'As you wish,' he said. 'But don't worry about clearing away. I'll do it.'

'You will?' Louise regarded him with suspicion. 'Or will you just stack it up in the kitchen for the maid?'

'My name,' he said gently, 'is not Marian Trentham.' He shook his head reprovingly as he refilled his glass. 'One of these days, I'm really going to have to teach you to trust me.'

She offered a constrained smile. 'Well—I'll be off, then.' And rose.

'Run away, if you must.' He raised his glass. 'Sweet dreams, Louise.' He paused, looking at her meditatively. 'I suppose you do dream?'

She halted in the doorway, looking back at him. He was leaning back in his chair, his face in shadow. 'Of course,' she said. 'Every night. I believe everyone does.'

'And what do you dream about?' he asked softly. 'Or is it a secret?'

Yes, she thought. My deepest, most intimate secret. Because I dream about you, Alex. About your arms around me, and your lips on mine. I dream that our marriage is a real one, and we're happier together than we could ever have imagined.

I dream that you want me, passionately.

And I know, at this moment, that if you were to give me just one sign—hold out your hand, speak my name—then I'd come to you here and now—tonight—and give myself forever.

But I also know that's the last thing on earth that you would

ever want. So I am indeed running away. Away from temptation. And heartbreak. Away from you.

She gave him a cool smile. 'I dream,' she said, 'about the
Taj Mahal. At sunset. What else? Goodnight, Alex.'

And went, not hurrying, down the corridor to the solitude
and safety of her own room.

CHAPTER EIGHT

'ARE you really sure about this?' Andie asked dubiously.

'If you mean—have I discussed it with Alex, then no,' said Louise, composedly tucking the card from the catering company in her bag.

'Well, don't you think you should?' Andie frowned a little. 'After all, he might not be too pleased to find his wife going round the City serving food to rival banks. Or even Perrins itself, God forbid. And he could have a point.'

Louise sighed. 'I have to do something,' she objected. 'I can't sit around all day wondering whether to have nail extensions or Botox.'

'Especially when you don't need either of them,' Andie agreed cordially. She paused. 'Of course, if you really want a time-consuming occupation, you could always take a leaf out of my book.'

'And become someone's PA?' Louise shook her head. 'I don't think I'm cut out for that.'

'It wasn't what I meant either.' Andie sat back in her chair, smiling. 'I wouldn't mention your proposed career in cooking to Alex until next week,' she added musingly. 'He's jumpy about this party you're going to tomorrow for some reason, and he's had one piece of bad news today already. We don't want an explosion, do we?'

'Bad news?' Louise was signalling to the waiter to bring the bill for their lunch. 'Why, what's happened?'

'I handed in my notice.'

'Oh, no.' Louise's distress was genuine. 'I thought you liked working for him. And, anyway, what am I going to do without you?'

'I do like working for him, and nothing's changed there. And

I hope you and I will continue to see each other.' Andie's sudden smile was shy and impish at the same time. 'Especially if you agree to be godmother.'

'Godmother,' Louise repeated on a rising note. 'You mean you're having a baby. Oh, Andie, that's wonderful.'

'I think so,' the other girl agreed. 'All I have to do now is convince Alex. I mean—he congratulated me and everything, but he looked as if he'd been poleaxed, and he's been really quiet all morning.' Her smile widened. 'Perhaps he's never associated marriage with babies before.'

'Probably not,' Louise agreed quietly.

'But now that he has, maybe he'll have his own ideas about your career path.'

Louise flushed at the other girl's teasing tone. 'Are—are you leaving the bank very soon?'

'Not really. I just thought I ought to warn him, so he can start looking for someone new. He is notoriously picky about close staff.' Andie glanced at her watch. 'I'd better get back before he fires me.'

'And I need to go home,' Louise added. 'My dress for the party is being delivered later on.'

'You sound as if they were bringing your shroud.' Andie patted her shoulder. 'You'll have a great time. After all, Alex is showing you off to the second most important woman in his life.'

'Really?' Louise smiled with an effort.

But who is the first? she asked herself with a pang as they emerged into the street, and the mini-heatwave that London was sweltering under. The one who shared our wedding night with him? Or someone else completely?

Aloud, she said brightly, 'Oh, good, there's a taxi coming. Shall I drop you at the bank?'

She chatted and laughed with Andie about her wonderful news until they reached Perrins, but once she was alone again Louise sank back into the corner of her seat, her face and thoughts equally wistful.

Lucky Andie, she told herself wearily. Married blissfully to a man who adored her, and now expecting his child.

The contrast between that and her own situation was almost too wretched to contemplate.

She had hoped so much that things might ease between Alex and herself after the night they had dinner together. That they might even be able to enjoy some kind of tenuous friendship. It wasn't what she wanted, of course, but it would have been better than nothing at all.

Yet, it seemed, she saw even less of him than before. He went out early each day, and came back very late each evening. But at least he did come back, she thought wryly.

And when their paths inevitably did cross, he was politely, even charmingly aloof. He could hardly have told her more strongly that there was no place for her in his life. That the rapport she'd thought was developing between them was simply a figment of her imagination.

I was a fool to hope, she thought with a silent sigh.

However, she might soon be put out of her misery. If things went well at the party this weekend, she might not even be around to be godmother to Andie's baby. She could instead be on the other side of the world, trying to put her life back together.

And her friendship with Andie would be another tie she would have to sever, she realised with real regret.

'Traffic's a nightmare, love,' the driver called back to her suddenly, breaking into her unhappy reverie. 'I'm going to try a short cut.' And he swung the cab down a narrow street lined with antique shops, and small galleries.

It was as the taxi slowed to negotiate its way round a delivery van that Louise caught sight of Alex.

For a moment, she thought she was dreaming. That he was so much in her thoughts that she could, apparently, conjure him up at will.

And then she saw he was not alone. That a woman was beside him, smiling up at him, her hand on his arm. And that they were standing on marble steps under the shade of a striped awning belonging to a hotel called the Belmayne, discreet and clearly exclusive.

It was like living through her worst nightmare, Louise thought, her throat contracting, as she recognised his companion's red hair. Registered the beautiful face with its confident, self-satisfied smile. And realised that her most terrible fears were finally being confirmed.

He said it was over, she thought with anguish. And I wanted to believe him, in spite of all the evidence to the contrary. Yet here they are together. And I can't fool myself any longer, or dream that I'll ever be of anything other than marginal importance to Alex.

Because he can't give Cindy Crosby up, no matter what the risk. Which proves how much he must care for her.

She wanted to cower down in her seat as if she was somehow the one in the wrong. The one who needed to escape attention.

He mustn't see me, she thought frantically. I can't bear it if he sees me. If he knows that I know…

It was a ludicrous reaction, and she knew it, but it was also totally instinctive.

She didn't want to provoke a confrontation in which she would almost inevitably come off the worst. In which she might break down and cry, or be guilty of some other act of self-betrayal.

After all, he had never promised to be faithful. Nor was he aware that he had the power to break her heart, she thought, swallowing back the tears burning in her throat. So at least she still had a measure of pride to sustain her through the remainder of their marriage. Which, she could only hope, would be mercifully brief. Because she was no longer sure how much more she could take.

She was thankful when her cab turned the corner, resisting the temptation to take one last look back.

Now she had to find the strength of will from somewhere to get through the coming weekend. To smile and pretend she was a happy, fulfilled wife. And the better she played her part, the sooner she might have her freedom, she reminded herself and paused, pain slashing at her.

Because she knew all too well that, no matter how many miles or months she was able to put between Alex and herself, she would never really be free of him.

That her unhappy, thankless love would keep her in his thrall for the rest of her life. And that was the secret burden she would have to bear, now and always.

Quite apart from the fevered state of her emotions, Louise felt unbearably hot and sticky when she got back to the flat.

Something cold to drink, she thought, kicking off her high-heeled sandals. And after that she'd take a shower.

She wandered barefoot into the kitchen and extracted a bottle of mineral water from the fridge, uncapping it and drinking thirstily, then placing the chilly glass against her forehead.

However much she was dreading the coming party, it would still be good to get out of the stifling city and breathe some country air, she thought, leaning against the counter-top. Maybe it would help her to think more clearly too.

She still wasn't sure what reception she would get from Lady Perrin. Alex had formally told his grandmother he was married, but so far there had been no reaction, and she wasn't sure if that was a good sign or bad. In fact she wasn't sure of very much at all except her own unhappiness, she thought, her heart like a stone in her chest.

As she tossed the empty bottle into the bin the door buzzer sounded, signalling that her dress had arrived, which was one less thing to worry about, she told herself, starting up the passage.

She had fallen in love with the deep red taffeta confection with its boned strapless bodice, and smooth bell of a skirt, as soon as she'd seen it. Its classic lines enhanced her slenderness, and the colour lent warmth to her pale skin, giving in turn a much-needed boost to her confidence.

She would never be Alex's wife in any real sense, she thought, but at least, for one night, she would look the part. And, if nothing else, she would make him proud of her.

She threw open the door, confidently expecting to see a messenger carrying a beribboned box. Instead she found herself taking a step backwards, her hand going to her throat.

She said, her voice sharp with disbelief, 'David?'

'Hello, Lou,' David Sanders said awkwardly. 'It's good to see you.'

She wished she could say the same, but it was impossible. She'd never expected to see him again. Never wanted to either, she realised.

She swallowed, taking a firm hold on herself. 'What are you doing here? How—how did you find me?'

'Ellie still had Fabian's address in her organiser,' he said. 'May I come in?'

She'd already responded with automatic politeness, standing to one side to admit him, before it struck her forcibly that it was the last thing she really wanted and that she should, instead, have told him to get lost.

Biting her lip, she followed him to the living room, where he stood looking around him appraisingly.

'Well,' he commented, 'you've certainly fallen on your feet.'

Louise was astounded to hear a faint note of injury in his voice. She gave him an inimical look. 'As opposed to flat on my face?' she queried. 'Or was that what you intended?'

'No, of course not,' he protested uncomfortably. He paused. 'Oh, God, Lou.' He shook his head. 'It's all such a bloody mess.'

'Is it?'

'You must know that it is. I've been such an idiot.'

Louise moved restively, regretting even more that she'd allowed him into the flat. And this was the man that, only a short time before, she had planned to marry. Now his presence was an embarrassment—a thorn in her side. How quickly things could change.

Anxious to be rid of him, she said, 'David, I have things to do. What do you want exactly?'

'I need to apologise,' he said intensely. 'To tell you that

going off with Ellie was the biggest mistake of my life, and beg you to forgive me.'

She shrugged. 'Consider yourself forgiven,' she told him curtly. 'Now, perhaps, you'll go. You should never have come here in the first place.'

'But we can't just leave it like that,' he objected. He sounded almost startled. 'You can't be happy, married to that bastard. And Ellie and I are through, or very nearly,' he added despondently. 'She and my mother can't stand the sight of each other, and she says my present salary is a joke, so she's insisting that I sell the house and get a job in London so that she can go back to work at Trentham Osborne.'

He sighed. 'She's changed completely. When we first met, she was so sweet—so fragile. I just fell—headlong. Now all she seems to think about is money. I suppose that's the result of associating with someone like Alex Fabian,' he added, giving his surroundings a look that combined envy with loathing.

Louise frowned. 'But she certainly didn't want to marry him,' she pointed out. 'She told me herself that he scared her.'

David shrugged. 'Maybe she's decided she'd rather be scared than bored,' he countered wanly. 'Or perhaps she was just miffed because Fabian had his own agenda, and wouldn't dance to her tune. Anyway, she certainly misses the high life. And she despises me because I can't afford to take her to the places he did.'

'I find that hard to believe.' Louise frowned. 'Although Alex has always said I didn't know Ellie as well as I thought.'

'Did any of us?' David asked glumly. 'Life's been sheer hell since we got back. My mother never stops complaining. Half my friends won't speak to me.'

'Am I supposed to feel sorry for you?'

'I can't expect that,' he said heavily. 'But hearing that you'd married Fabian was simply the final straw. Something—died in me, I think.'

'That sounds like a line from the drama group's last production,' Louise told him coldly. 'And my marriage is no concern of yours.'

'But you're so wrong.' He gave her a pathetic look. 'We had a good thing going for us, Lou. We could have made it. Besides,' he added, with a startling shift in direction, 'what are you going to do when Fabian gets tired of you, and you're kicked into touch?'

'Oh, that's all settled,' she said over-brightly, resisting the impulse to wrap defensive arms round her body and howl. 'I shall travel the world as a rich divorcee.'

'But not alone,' he said quickly. 'You'll never need to do that, Lou.'

She stared at him open-mouthed. 'You surely can't be suggesting yourself as travelling companion?'

'Why not?' His voice was eager. 'I've admitted I've been a fool, and that must count for something. So, Lou—darling Lou—why shouldn't we make a fresh start?'

She said wearily, 'For more reasons than I care to enumerate. And my name is Louise. My husband prefers it.'

'Husband,' he said with contempt. 'He's no more a husband to you than he would have been to Ellie.'

'And you,' Louise flashed back, 'know only what Ellie's told you.' She went to the door. 'David, I think you should leave. Now.'

'I've upset you,' he said. 'Just turning up like this. I should have written to you, or rung first, but I was just so desperate to see you—to put things right. Because I know that, if you give me the chance, I can make you happy.'

'On the contrary,' Louise said coldly. 'I think we've both had a lucky escape.' She paused, adding levelly, 'You need to remember, David, that you and Ellie were sufficiently in love a few weeks ago to run away together. You may just be going through a bad patch at the moment.'

'It was just a silly infatuation,' David said. 'I see that now.'

Louise moved restively. 'Whatever,' she said. 'I'm really not interested.'

'Sweetheart,' he said coaxingly, 'you don't mean that. You can't have forgotten what we were to each other.'

'A habit,' she said, 'that is now broken. So let's leave it like that.'

'But how can I,' he demanded, 'when you're the only woman I'm ever going to want? Please don't send me away, Lou. I should never have let you go, and I know that, given the chance, I can make it work. You look amazing,' he added huskily.

'The only amazing thing about me is that I'm actually listening to this drivel.' Louise marched to the front door and flung it open, standing beside it, stony-faced.

'My God,' he said. 'I never thought you could be so hard. That's what he's done to you, isn't it?'

'A few other factors were also involved.' She lifted her chin. 'Goodbye, David.'

He gave her one last sorrowful look, and left. Louise closed the door behind him with deliberate firmness, and stood for a moment looking at its blank panels.

I should be in a terrible state, she thought. The man I planned to marry has just grovelled to me, and begged me to go back to him. And, in view of what I know about Alex, I should be at least—torn. And yet I know beyond all doubt that I wouldn't have David back, if he came gift-wrapped, with a cash bonus.

She began to unzip her pale yellow linen dress as she walked down to her room. She adjusted the shower temperature to cool, then stripped off her underwear and stepped under the refreshing torrent of water, letting it cascade over her hair, and down her body.

David wanted her, and Alex never would. There was a terrible irony in that, she thought, lifting her face so that the power-driven droplets mingled with the tears she could no longer hold back. Standing motionless until she had regained some measure of control.

When she'd dried herself, and given her hair a swift towelling, she slipped on her white broderie-anglaise robe. It was pointless trying to alter the immutable, she thought. She would only become more hurt than she was already.

Far better to devote herself to practicalities like packing for the weekend. And telephoning the shop about her dress, which should be here by now, she reminded herself.

Still barefoot, she went up the hallway to the living room, only to come to an abrupt halt in the doorway. It was a day for shocks, she thought, swallowing. Because Alex was there, standing on the other side of the room by the window, his back towards her.

She was all set to beat a retreat, convinced she hadn't made a sound, but he turned instantly, his brows snapping together as he surveyed her.

Louise returned his gaze, her chin lifted. She had no idea what could have brought him back at this time in the afternoon—unless, of course, he'd come to tell her that their token marriage was over. That he and Cindy Crosby could no longer bear to live apart.

Please God, don't let me grovel like David, she whispered silently. Don't let me beg for mercy. Isn't it bad enough that I'm standing here with bare feet and damp hair?

That too potent image of them standing together on the steps of the hotel where they'd been making love flashed into her mind, and flooded her face with indignant, painful colour.

But anger was good. Anger was infinitely safer than hurt—and need.

The green eyes narrowed. He said softly, 'Hello, darling. You seem—surprised to see me.'

'I was having a shower. I didn't hear you come in.' She hesitated. 'And you're quite right. I wasn't expecting you.'

'I hope my return hasn't inconvenienced you in any way.' His tone was silky.

'This is your home,' Louise returned. 'You're entitled to come and go as you please. I thought we'd established that.'

'Do you usually take showers in the middle of the afternoon?'

'Sometimes, when it's as hot as this.' Absurd to feel defensive, yet she did, just the same. 'Why do you ask?'

He shrugged, his smile glittering at her like ice. 'Just natural curiosity, my sweet, about how you spend your time when I'm not around.'

'I could ask you the same thing,' she countered.

'Then why don't you?'

She bit her lip. 'Perhaps because I already know the answer.' She was on thin ice, but she couldn't help herself.

'I wonder if you do,' he murmured.

There was an odd silence, and a tension in the air that made her skin tingle suddenly.

Could he actually be feeling concern about telling her his decision? she wondered. Yet the vibrations she was picking up seemed in some strange way to be more angry than anxious. As if he was controlling his temper with immense effort.

Louise felt as if she was on the scaffold waiting for the axe to fall, and decided she couldn't bear it any longer. That she had to force an open confrontation, whatever the cost.

She swallowed. 'Did—did you come back for a particular reason?' She paused, trying to read his expression and failing. 'You—you have something you want to say to me?'

'Perhaps,' he said. 'But it will keep for another time.'

He walked across the room, tossing his discarded jacket over the arm of a chair, loosening his tie. He sat down on one of the sofas, stretching long legs in front of him with apparent indolence. But still, she realised, watching her with that hooded, enigmatic gaze. Making her suspect that, under the relaxed pose, he was really as tense as a coiled spring.

He said, 'Is that a new dressing gown?'

'I bought it last week.' *And why are we discussing trivialities like this? Why don't you tell me what's really on your mind?*

'Ah,' Alex said. 'I thought I hadn't seen it before. Because I'm sure I should have remembered such a charming—and seductive piece of nonsense.'

He was smiling as he spoke, and she had to fight an impulse to tighten the sash round her slender waist, wishing with all her heart that she were fully dressed. Because his smile, and the cool, watchful intensity of his stare, was beginning to alarm her.

'But then,' she returned with a creditable assumption of calm, 'you're here so seldom these days.'

'Yes,' he said softly. 'And that has clearly been a mistake which I shall have to rectify.' He paused. 'And, as I'm here now, why don't you sit down and let us enjoy a pleasant marital chat, the way that husbands and wives do?'

'Because we don't really fall within that category.' Louise tried to speak lightly. To ignore the fact that she was shaking inside. 'Also, I have things to do.'

'Ah,' he said, his brows lifting. 'And, no doubt, places to go, and people to see.'

'I'm going away with you,' she said. 'To meet your grandmother, and assure her that you've turned into a model husband. So I need to pack.' She touched her dry lips with the tip of her tongue. 'Also to call the shop and ask why my dress for her party hasn't arrived yet.'

'Nothing too urgent, then,' he said. He pointed to the sofa opposite. 'So, join me.' His smile glinted at her. 'Or do I have to fetch you?'

No, she thought. He certainly did not have to do that.

She obeyed reluctantly, sitting bolt upright, carefully arranging her broderie-anglaise skirts around her legs with nervous hands.

Alex leaned back, lacing his fingers behind his head. 'You seem on edge, my sweet,' he remarked. 'Do you find my presence so daunting?'

She shrugged defensively. 'No—I'm still a little taken aback to find you here in the middle of a working day.'

'Perhaps I felt in need of some female company,' he drawled. 'Is that so surprising?'

Hurt wrenched at her. If that was indeed the case, why hadn't he stayed with Cindy Crosby, as he'd had every opportunity to do?

She sent him a burning look. 'Astonishing, frankly.' She paused. 'I can't imagine I'd be your first choice for that, or even on the A list.'

'You do yourself an injustice, darling.' He looked back at her meditatively. 'So—tell me about your day.'

Louise fidgeted with a fold of her skirt. 'I hardly think you'd be interested.'

'Try me,' he invited softly. 'Run through some of the highlights. The key moments.'

Oh, God, Louise thought, her throat tightening. He must have spotted me in that taxi. He knows that I saw him—that I'm well aware he's still Cindy Crosby's lover, and he wants to know what I'm going to do about it. He needs to check my reaction, in case I'm planning to be trouble.

She ticked off on her fingers. 'I got up after you left. I had breakfast. I put on a yellow dress that you also haven't seen. And I had lunch with Andie.' She forced a smile. 'It's great news about the baby, isn't it?'

'The best,' he said. 'And after lunch?'

'I came home.' No, she thought, in truth I came back to this expensive, luxurious shell which merely masquerades as a home. 'And the rest you know,' she went on, trying for insouciance. 'Not exactly world-shattering, is it?'

'That might depend,' Alex said slowly, 'on how you see your world. But is that really all, my sweet? You're sure you haven't forgotten something? Some—encounter, maybe?'

She could not believe he was being so cruel. That he could actually taunt her with the knowledge that he was still Cindy Crosby's lover.

Her hands clenched together in her lap, as she fought an inward battle for calm, and courage. 'If I have,' she said, keeping her voice level, 'it's because it's really not important. Because it doesn't alter the essence of the bargain we made.'

She lifted her chin. 'We—we are both free agents, at least in private. And nothing that's happened is going to change the way I behave towards you in public this weekend. I promise you that. I'll—play my part, as agreed. You'll have nothing to complain about.'

There was a long, deafening silence, then Alex said quietly, 'I see. Then may I suggest that next time you decide to entertain your lover for a little afternoon delight, you warn me in advance? I'd hate to be guilty of some tactless intrusion—as I might have been today.'

'My lover?' Louise repeated, stunned. 'What are you talking about?'

'I saw the lift come down from the penthouse,' he said, 'and David Sanders leave it. And please don't tell me I made a mistake, because I recognised him from the photograph in your bedroom at the cottage.

'He was naturally far too preoccupied to notice me,' he added bitingly. 'But then I'm certain you'd assured him I was safely at work a few miles away, so he wouldn't have expected to see me. Any more than you did, my sweet.'

He paused. 'A word of advice. Avoid taking a bath or shower in the middle of the day. It tends to arouse suspicion.' His smile was hard. 'Besides, it's not essential. I'm hardly likely to taste him on your skin, am I, darling?'

Her head fell back in shock, as if he'd struck her.

'You—you are daring to accuse me?' Her voice was low and trembling. 'You think David came here—for that?'

'It's a fair assumption,' he said coldly. 'When I find you here, the picture of guilt, and next-door to naked. Did you choose the dressing gown specially, my sweet? Does he prefer the virginal look—especially when it only consists of a layer of fabric?'

The anger was out in the open now. The words bitter—corrosive.

Louise bit her lip. 'Believe what you wish,' she returned equally icily. 'But I was fully dressed when David arrived. And there was no prior arrangement, either. I thought he was the messenger delivering my dress, or I wouldn't have opened the door.'

'You're claiming he simply turned up out of the blue?' Alex asked with derision. 'How did he know where to find you?'

'Apparently he looked up your address in Ellie's organiser.' She hesitated. 'He came to tell me—things hadn't worked out between them.'

'What a bloody surprise,' he said contemptuously. 'Was that all he said?'

'No.' Louise stared at the floor. 'He—he wants me to go back to him.'

'How touching,' Alex said blightingly. 'So when's your next assignation? And please don't have him in my bed, darling, because I wouldn't find that amusing.'

'I wouldn't dream of it,' Louise hurled back at him, riled beyond endurance. 'I was thinking we might try the Belmayne Hotel instead. Would you recommend it?'

The sudden silence seemed to stretch into eternity.

At last he said grimly, 'What the hell are you talking about?'

'About your damned hypocrisy.' She was on her feet, shaking like a leaf. 'I saw you, Alex. I saw you with your friend, Mrs Crosby. Your love nest is on a cab drivers' rat run. And I know the name of the rat!'

'Why, Louise,' he said softly, 'if I didn't know better I'd say you were jealous.' He paused. 'So what happens now? I expect the gutter Press would pay handsomely for the information.'

'I'm sure they would,' she hit back. 'But I prefer to make you pay—when all this is over. When I'm free, and you're sharing Rosshampton with the beautiful Mrs Crosby. She already has a country house, so a mansion is clearly the next logical step.'

She turned abruptly, making the broderie-anglaise skirts swirl around her, and marched to the door. 'And now I'm going to my room, to pack for our weekend of wedded bliss. Please let me know when my dress arrives.'

She was at the door when his voice reached her, quiet, but with an odd raw note. 'Louise—tell me the truth. Is David Sanders your lover?'

She looked back at him over her shoulder, her mouth twisting. 'Why, Alex.' She kept her own tone light, even mocking. 'If I didn't know better, I'd say you were jealous.'

She left the room, her head held high. And only she knew that her heart was weeping.

CHAPTER NINE

THEY drove down to Rosshampton the following afternoon, having reached what Louise could only wearily suppose, was a state of armed neutrality.

She had gone to her room, the day before, and stayed there, and he had made no attempt to follow. And she hadn't cried, because she couldn't allow herself to do that. Not again. Not yet.

But one day soon, when she was finally and completely alone, she would let herself grieve for a love that had never been hers.

Instead she had begun to pack for the weekend, moving like an automaton, trying to recall what Alex had told her about its format.

They would be expected to arrive in time for tea, and in the evening there would be a small dinner for family and a few close friends.

The real celebration would be the birthday party on Saturday night, when she would dance in Alex's arms for the first and last time, wearing her new dress, which had finally arrived an hour later.

Alex had tapped on the door. 'There's a package for you.'

'Oh, thank you.' She took a deep breath, then walked to the door and opened it. He handed her the flat striped box, but as she made to close the door again, he stopped her, his expression faintly quizzical.

'Don't I get to see it?'

'Don't you trust my judgement?' Louise parried.

He shrugged. 'Trust hasn't played a great part in this relationship so far.'

'We don't have a relationship,' she said. 'We have a deal.'

141

'Just the same,' he said. 'May I look?'

Reluctantly Louise lifted the lid of the box, parting the sheets of protective tissue. She took out the shimmering folds of dark red taffeta, and held them against herself, briefly and self-consciously.

'Will it do?' She didn't look at him.

'Yes,' he said, after a pause. 'It will do very well. Thank you.'

He turned and walked away, and she closed the door behind him and leaned against it, aware that her breathing had quickened.

A short while later, she heard him go out, and she had not seen him again until this afternoon, when he had returned to collect her for the journey down to Rosshampton.

She had assumed that Alex would be driving himself, as he'd done when they first met, and had to hide her disappointment when he told her that he had decided to use the limousine and his driver as he had work to do on the journey. This meant that there would be no real chance to talk, and maybe even reach some much-needed rapprochement before they arrived for the party.

Harry, Alex's driver, was polite and pleasant, and she liked him. She also knew there was no way he could overhear any passenger conversations, but that did not prevent her feeling absurdly self-conscious when he was present.

Besides, she thought with an inward sigh, there was no guarantee that she and Alex would discuss the events of the past twenty-four hours any more calmly and rationally than they had done already, and it would only take Harry one glance in the mirror to see they were having a row.

So maybe it was better this way, she thought, sitting on opposite sides of the car and concentrating on anything except each other.

He'd courteously offered her the *Financial Times*, and she'd declined with equal politeness.

Now, while Alex studied the papers he'd taken from his briefcase, Louise turned away from his cool, uncompromising profile and stared resolutely out of the window at the passing scenery, reviewing in her mind what he'd told her in the past about the South African connection.

Cliff Maidstone, she thought, grandson of a man that Selina Perrin might once have wanted to marry, but who'd been sent abroad to avoid prosecution after some trouble over money. Accompanied by Della, his wife of less than a year and a former model. Described himself as an investment adviser. No apparent shortage of funds, or charm. Loud in his praise of Rosshampton, which had been lovingly described to him, as a small child, by his grandfather. Had numerous memories to share with Lady Perrin of times when Archie Maidstone had stayed at the house himself.

'The man's clever,' Alex had commented tersely. 'Apparently, he's mentioned his grandfather's lifelong regret for the "stupidity" that drove him away from everything he held dear. Which, of course, includes Selina.'

He gave a sigh of exasperation. 'What woman wouldn't like to think she was some man's lifelong regret?'

'It's not something that would appeal to me,' Louise said.

But then, she thought sadly, she had her own regrets that might very well last a lifetime.

She cleared her throat. 'How—how have you found out all these things?'

He shrugged. 'Major rule in business. Know your enemy.'

'And presumably,' Louise said quietly, 'your enemy also knows you.'

'Ah,' Alex said with a swift, crooked grin. 'But I have a secret weapon in you, my sweet.'

But will I be enough? Louise asked herself, remembering the exchange. Supposing his grandmother doesn't like me—or has already put two and two together and realises this marriage is simply a put-up job?

She realised suddenly that the car was slowing and turning in between two tall stone pillars, and on, up a long sweep of drive.

Then the house was in front of them, a gracious sprawl of

grey stone and mullioned windows, and she forgot everything else as she had her first view of Rosshampton.

It looked, she thought with sudden wonder, as if it had been there forever, framed by trees, as ancient and mellow as the landscape itself that surrounded it. The lawns seemed almost sculptured in their perfection, and the waters of the lake sparkled with blue and gold in the distance.

It was a house totally at ease with itself, and with its past, and she could understand for the first time why Alex loved it so much and desired it so fiercely that he was prepared to go to any lengths to acquire it.

Could understand—and almost sympathise.

She knew, too, that she would move heaven and earth to help him achieve his dream, if it was at all possible. That it would be her gift of love to him. The first, and also the last.

'Well?'

She started a little at the sound of his voice. Turned to see him regarding her with a faint smile.

'It's so beautiful,' she said slowly. 'I never thought it would be like this.' Or that I—I'd want it too, she added silently. Because that was something he would not want to hear. There was no place for her in Alex's future plans. So much so that he was prepared to pay a fortune for her to go away, she reminded herself, straightening her shoulders and reaching for her bag. And she could not let herself forget that even for a minute.

The car drew to a halt in front of an imposing main entrance, where a man neatly dressed in a dark suit was waiting to greet them.

'That's Gillow,' Alex told her in an undertone as they left the car. 'He and his wife run the place, with additional help when they need it. They've been with Selina for years, and meeting you is going to be a big moment for them. Mrs Gillow has been asking for years when I'm going to meet a nice young lady. Almost from the time I left school, in fact.'

She winced. 'Now, why does that make me feel no better about all this?'

'Want to pull out?'

'No,' she said, lifting her chin. 'I came to do a job, and I'll do it.'

He said, 'Then it begins.' He took her hand, and she walked beside him, smiling, into the house.

Lady Perrin was in the drawing room, seated in a corner of one of the brocaded sofas that flanked the fireplace.

'Grandmother,' Alex said, leading her forward. 'This is Louise—my wife.'

Lady Perrin's shrewd gaze swept over her, taking in every detail of the plain taupe dress, the dark brown patent shoes and bag, the gold studs in her ears and, more particularly, the plain band on her wedding finger. She gave a slight nod.

'So,' she said, 'you're the girl who's managed to tame my grandson at last.'

'Oh, no, Lady Perrin,' Louise said serenely. 'I wouldn't even attempt to do that. I think he's pretty wonderful just the way he is.'

'Then you must be very easy to please,' the older woman said tartly. She patted the sofa beside her. 'Sit down, child, and tell me something about yourself. Alexander has been distressingly reticent. I think he wanted to surprise me, and he has.'

She turned to him. 'You need not wait, Alexander. Gillow will have taken your bags up to the Chinese Room.'

'The Chinese Room?' Alex repeated, an odd note in his voice. 'Not the Royal Suite?'

'I've given that to the Maidstones on this occasion,' his grandmother told him affably. 'I knew you wouldn't mind.'

'No, of course not.' Alex's face and tone were expressionless. 'The Chinese Room it is, then.'

'I'll send your wife to you when we've had our little chat.' She gave him a thin smile. 'You have better taste than I thought, grandson.'

Louise sat down, folding her hands in her lap, drawing on every atom of composure she possessed.

She was expecting the latter-day equivalent of the Spanish Inquisition from this formidable old lady, but once they were alone Lady Perrin became far more friendly. Her questions about Louise's family, education and former career were certainly probing, but they were also kind, and she appeared genuinely interested.

And she seemed to accept without demur Louise's calm explanation that she'd met Alex while he was negotiating a finance deal with her father.

'It's almost the truth, after all,' Alex had pointed out. 'So why invent another story?'

'It's no wonder that he snapped you up with such indecent haste,' Lady Perrin was saying. 'I did wonder—but no matter.' She paused. 'Tell me, my dear, does he make you happy?'

Louise hadn't been expecting that. The older woman had slipped it under her guard, and for a moment she almost faltered, then she made herself look up, and meet Lady Perrin's eyes. She even managed to smile.

She said calmly, 'He's made me love him more than I dreamed I would ever be able to care for anyone.'

'That is not,' said Lady Perrin, 'what I asked, but never mind. Alexander is a very fortunate man.' She glanced at her watch. 'Now go upstairs and join him. Mrs Gillow will show you the way. Tea will be in half an hour, when the Maidstones return from their walk in the garden.'

And Louise found herself dismissed.

On the way upstairs, a clearly delighted Mrs Gillow regaled her with stories about Alex's boyhood. At any other time Louise would have gobbled them up, but a slight feeling of uneasiness was stirring inside her. Alex had been so definite that they would be given the Royal Suite, yet it seemed they'd been put somewhere else. And what were the implications of that? she asked herself, remembering his reaction.

She did not have to wait long to find out. Mrs Gillow opened a door with a flourish, and Louise stepped forward into the Chinese Room.

She could see at once how it had acquired its name. It was a large room, overlooking the lake, its walls covered in a charming oriental paper, and the eastern theme was repeated in the tall porcelain vases that graced the mantelpiece. There were washed Chinese rugs on the polished wood floor, and the window hangings were dull gold, as was the quilted coverlet on the room's only bed.

It was that which caught the eye of course. Focused her appalled attention. It was a very wide bed—kingsize or even larger—but it stood in solitary splendour, everything about it suggesting double occupation.

Which was not, and never had been, part of the deal, Louise thought, her throat tightening uncontrollably.

As she heard the door close behind Mrs Gillow, Louise looked across the room to where Alex was standing by the window.

She said huskily, 'What is this?' Her voice rose. 'You said two rooms. You promised me...'

He shrugged. 'You heard what Selina said. She's given the Royal Suite to the Maidstones. A great mark of favour,' he added drily.

'But she can't.' Louise wrapped defensive arms round her body. 'And we can't either—share this room, I mean.'

'Unfortunately, we don't have a choice,' Alex drawled. 'But it's a very big bed and, although I don't have a naked sword to place between us in the true spirit of chivalry, a couple of those pillows should provide sufficient deterrent.'

'No,' she said, her heart thudding unevenly. 'No, I won't do it.' She pointed to a door. 'What's in there?'

'A bathroom.'

'Problem solved,' she said. 'You could sleep in the bath.'

'Indeed, I could,' he said cordially. 'I could also dangle from the light fitting. But I'm not going to. I intend to spend the night in that bed.'

There was a chaise longue in the window alcove, with a gilded sleeping dragon curled along its back. She pointed to it. 'You can use that.'

'Forget it,' he said tersely. 'Quite apart from being seriously uncomfortable, the damned thing is only about five feet long.

I, on the other hand, am over six feet tall, in case you hadn't noticed,' he added witheringly.

She lifted her chin angrily. 'Then I shall sleep there myself.'

'Fine.' He shrugged. 'That's your decision—and your funeral.' His mouth slanted. 'Or you'll wish it was after a few hours on that bloody couch.'

She was close to furious, frightened tears. Her voice shook. 'You planned this deliberately, didn't you?'

'Oh, sure,' Alex said derisively. 'I can just hear myself. "Oh, Gran, my wife won't sleep with me, so can you—throw us together somehow? If we're in the same bed, I can maybe talk her round."' He snorted. 'Get real, Louise.'

'But there must be something we can do.'

'There is,' he said. 'We can accept the situation. And I've already started.' He pointed to the wardrobe. 'I hung up your dress.'

'Thank you,' she said stonily.

'Think nothing of it,' he returned. 'As I'm sure you already do.' He paused, then said more gently, 'I'll try and make the situation as easy as I can for you. Ensure that you have privacy while you're changing. Take care not to walk into the bathroom without knocking. And make sure that the lights are off when I come to bed,' he added drily. 'Because I don't wear pyjamas.'

She stared down at the polished floor, aware that her face had warmed. 'Very well.' Her voice was muffled as she tried to erase from her mind an unwanted image of how Alex would look without his clothes.

'And after all,' he added, 'it's only for a couple of nights. Then you'll have all your own space again.' He gave her a brief smile. 'Now, we'd better go down and have tea with Selina.'

The Maidstones were already in the drawing room when they got there. He was tall and broad-shouldered, with dark hair and hot brown eyes in a ruddy face. Della Maidstone was a willowy blonde with a kittenish expression. They smiled lovingly at each other, showing very white teeth, and touched a lot, too, and Louise found herself quite irrationally disliking them intensely.

Surely Lady Perrin couldn't really think that they were suitable custodians for Rosshampton, she thought in bewilderment.

Yet she seemed to be surveying their antics benignly enough. Cliff Maidstone treated her with a combination of flirtatiousness and respect that she seemed to enjoy, and Della talked brightly about the celebrities she'd met during her modelling career.

Louise was almost certain that Lady Perrin had no idea who most of them were, but she listened to Della's revelations with an air of keen interest.

'I do miss my career,' the younger woman admitted eventually, with a sigh. She looked at Louise. 'Do you have a job, Mrs Fabian?'

'Not at the moment,' Louise responded. 'But I'm thinking of going into corporate catering,' she added, avoiding Alex's swift, narrow-eyed glance.

Della's blue eyes widened. 'You mean complicated cooking and stuff.' She shook her head. 'I can burn boiled water, can't I, Cliffy?'

He laughed heartily. 'You're not that bad, sweet thing.' He turned to Alex. 'So your wife's a great cook, is she?'

'My wife does everything well,' Alex returned silkily. 'She manages to surprise me on a daily basis.'

Louise selected a cucumber sandwich, and bit it—hard.

'Of course, you two are still on your honeymoon,' Della put in suddenly. 'Did you have a wonderful, romantic wedding? I loved every minute of mine,' she went on, fortunately not waiting for an answer, and launched herself into a detailed description, involving yards of tulle, number of layers on the wedding cake, average age of bridesmaids, multitude of guests in attendance, and the hilarious thing her sister's child had said at the evening barbecue and dance which had rounded off the celebrations.

Louise, brain reeling, met, unwisely, the glint of unholy

amusement in Alex's eyes, and was almost betrayed into a giggle.

She was thankful when Della eventually ran out of steam, and the awkward meal came to an end. She found herself left to her own devices, Lady Perrin having stated imperiously that she wished a private word with Alex in the library, prompting the Maidstones to exchange uneasy glances.

Louise made haste to escape to the garden. It was still slumberously warm, the bees industrious in the flower borders, birdsong muted with the approach of evening.

This was what she needed, she told herself, drawing in lungfuls of fragrant air as she headed for the lake.

The prospect of the night ahead was hanging over her like a deep shadow. Sleeping with him just across the hallway at the flat had been a disturbing enough experience. The thought of having to share a room, however platonically, was almost unbearable.

But only to me, she thought. It clearly doesn't worry him in the slightest. And if I needed proof of his total indifference to me, then I have it now.

There were no visible marks, of course, but she was hurting—bleeding—just the same. And she would carry the hidden scars forever.

As she reached the edge of the lake, a pair of swans emerged from the reeds and began to move slowly and gracefully across the sunlit water.

She stood watching them for a while, shading her eyes with her hand. They mate for life, she thought, which is something I don't need to contemplate right now. And she turned her back on them, and walked swiftly on.

If tea had been difficult, dinner proved to be a nightmare. Louise found herself seated next to Cliff Maidstone, and had to endure some heavy-handed joshing on Alex's reputation as a playboy—'Let's hope he's reformed, eh?'—before he moved on to the subject of Rosshampton.

'Of course, I regard the place as almost a second home now,' he told her with open satisfaction. 'Lady Perrin has been extremely gracious with her invitations, and I knew she'd take to my little Della right away. In fact,' here he lowered his voice confidentially, 'I have to say she's treated us as if we were her guests of honour.'

'So when are you planning to go back to South Africa?' Louise asked coolly, as soon as he paused for breath.

He gave her a smug grin. 'Let's just say my plans are—fluid at the moment. The old lady and my grandfather were pretty close at one time, and I guess I remind her of him.

'The family didn't want to know about him, of course. They were pushing her to marry another cousin—a Perrin, naturally. One of those convenient business mergers, and to hell with the bride's feelings. Incredible, eh?'

'Amazing,' said Louise.

The food was delicious but it was turning to ashes in her mouth, she reflected, watching Della bat her long eyelashes at Alex on the other side of the table.

Most of Lady Perrin's other guests were on the elderly side, so once coffee had been drunk in the drawing room they began to make their excuses and drift away home. Then the Maidstones, who'd been concealing their yawns for half an hour, said their goodnights and went upstairs.

'You look tired too, child.' Lady Perrin gave Louise a penetrating look. 'Run off to bed. I promise I won't keep your husband away from you for too long.' She lifted a scented cheek. 'You may kiss me, my dear.'

Louise, obeying, realised that she had no choice but to accept her dismissal, and went reluctantly up to the Chinese Room.

She had cornered Mrs Gillow earlier and asked for an extra blanket, much to the good woman's surprise, and this was now lying neatly folded on the bed.

Louise took the blanket, and one of the pillows, and transferred them to the chaise longue. She had considered sleeping fully dressed, but knew that this would merely subject her to derisive remarks from Alex, so she had no alternative other than to change into the nightdress in primrose voile which was the only night attire she'd brought with her.

But at least she'd be wearing something, she thought, biting her lip.

Her make-up removed and her hair brushed, she came back into the bedroom, eyeing her makeshift bed with misgivings. Perhaps some air would help her sleep, she thought, and went to the window. As she pushed the casement open she heard the sound of voices from the terrace below, and realised Alex must be walking there with his grandmother.

At that moment, Lady Perrin's precise tones came floating up to her with total clarity. 'The Crosby woman, Alex. I trust that she belongs completely in the past.'

There was a pause, then Alex's voice, quiet, almost sombre, reached her too. He said, 'I'm afraid, Gran, I'm not finding it quite that simple.'

What was it they said about eavesdroppers? Louise thought desolately, closing the window noiselessly again. She would rather do without fresh air than listen to any further revelations about the woman Alex loved, and his inability to give her up. And she was astonished that he should be making them to his grandmother, anyway.

Unless of course she'd guaranteed that Rosshampton would be his, and he'd decided he ought to be frank about the identity of its future mistress.

She lay down on the chaise longue, wrapping the blanket awkwardly round her and trying to find a comfortable position. Alex, she thought, had not been joking about this horrid piece of furniture.

She'd wanted very much to be asleep when he came to bed, but she was still wide awake when he came softly into the room half an hour later.

True to his word, he switched off the lights, but Louise closed her eyes tightly just the same, and lay like a stone. The rest of her senses seemed curiously heightened in the darkness. She could hear, she realised, the rustle of his clothes as he removed them. Could remember the taste of his mouth on hers.

Could feel the rougher texture of the blanket grazing her skin through the delicate fabric of her nightgown as if it did not exist, and the swift, involuntary hardening of her nipples in response.

Her whole body seemed alive, stirring—curious.

And suddenly he was there, beside her, standing over her in the shadows. The warm, clean scent of his skin was all around her, making the breath catch in her throat.

Because she knew that he was waiting for some sign. That all she had to do was open her eyes—reach out a hand to touch him.

No, she thought, *I won't—I can't...*

Tiny sparks danced behind her desperately closed lids. She made herself breathe slowly and evenly in a pretence of deep sleep.

And heard him say quietly, 'Goodnight, Louise.'

Telling her plainly that she hadn't fooled him for a second. Then he was gone, and she was aware, even from across the room, of the slight sound of the mattress dipping beneath his weight.

And she turned over, dragging the recalcitrant blanket with her, and buried her burning face in the pillow.

CHAPTER TEN

LOUISE was aware, even before she opened her eyes the next morning, that something was wrong.

That her body was no longer aching from the effort of trying to adapt to that unrelenting couch, or her skin being scratched by the blanket.

That she was, in fact, almost blissfully comfortable. Even though she did not seem to be lying on a pillow.

Very slowly and carefully she raised her eyelids, and paused, her body shuddering into shocked tension. Because the chaise longue was empty and abandoned on the other side of the room. And she was lying in the bed, in the curve of Alex's arm, with her head on his shoulder.

'Oh, no,' she whispered in silent horror. 'It can't be true. It *can't*. Did he come and take me, or did I go to him? Oh, God, why can't I remember?'

At any rate, she appeared to be still wearing her nightgown. And surely she'd know if—anything had happened between them?

Alex seemed to be deeply, genuinely asleep, so she began to ease herself away from the compelling warmth of his body. To extricate herself from the situation while she could.

Only to have him murmur a drowsy protest and scoop her back into his embrace.

Louise decided she was finished with subtlety. She had to get out of this bed right now.

She resolutely removed the hand that was clasping her hip with such dangerous intimacy, and was wriggling across to the edge of the bed when he lifted his head from the pillow and focused sleepy eyes on her.

'Good morning,' he said, yawning. 'I hope you slept well.'

'Exactly what am I doing here?' Her voice was husky.

'You were crying out in your sleep,' he said. 'A bad dream, perhaps. And you'd kicked off the blanket, so you were freezing too. I thought you'd be better off sleeping with me.'

He paused. 'And sleep you did, my love.'

'Do you really expect me to believe that you brought me here for my own good?' Her voice shook.

Alex propped himself on an elbow. He said levelly, 'Louise, you were in trouble—even sobbing at one point. You seemed to need something—someone. And I was all there was.'

'I need to know exactly what happened between us last night.'

His smile glinted at her. 'You were a tigress,' he said softly. 'A revelation.'

For a heartbeat, she almost believed him, then she saw the smile slide into a grin of pure enjoyment.

'Darling,' he said, 'if I'd made love to you last night, you'd have been well aware of the fact this morning. As it was, you curled up against me as if you belonged there.'

'I had no idea what I was doing,' she countered.

'No?' His brows lifted. 'And yet when I was carrying you across the room, you said my name.'

Louise's heart skipped a beat. 'Well,' she said, 'I only have your word for that.' She paused. 'What happened next?'

'We slept,' Alex said. 'Nothing more.'

He stretched, powerfully, lazily, making her vividly aware of the strong play of muscle under the smooth skin. She found she was watching him as if mesmerised, her mouth suddenly dry.

'Although that could always change,' he added casually, 'if you wanted. And right now,' the green eyes met hers, 'do you—want?'

'No.' She remembered, with a pang, the snatch of conversation she'd heard the night before. She bent her head. 'I—I suppose that's where men and women differ. A man can want sex even if he's in love with someone else.'

'What pigs we all are,' Alex said cordially. 'But you, of

course, being female and therefore purer and nobler, could not compromise your principles. Tell me, is it lonely up there on the moral high ground, sweetheart?'

Hurriedly, Louise began to push back the covers. 'I must get up now.'

'No,' he said. 'Not yet. It's still very early, and there are a few matters we need to discuss.'

'Then can we postpone the conversation until later, when we're both dressed?' she asked tautly.

'On the contrary,' he said. 'We can enjoy some pillow talk like other couples, even if a little recreational sex is out of the question. So don't run away, Louise, because I'd only come after you, and who knows where that might lead?' he added mockingly.

She flushed mutinously, but remained where she was. It seemed safer that way, even though her whole body was still tingling in half-shamed excitement at the thought of having spent the night in his arms, and common sense suggested she should distance herself from him, and fast.

She felt suddenly vulnerable in her flimsy nightdress, so she drew the coverlet over her body again. 'What do you want to say?'

'I need to apologise to you,' he said. 'So listen carefully, because it won't happen often.' He paused. 'I made certain accusations yesterday about your behaviour. These were purely circumstantial, and obviously had no basis in fact. Because I know quite well that David Sanders is not, and never has been your lover.' His mouth twisted ruefully. 'But appearances can be deceptive, so I lost my temper, and I'm sorry.'

'Then why did you?' Louise looked down at her tightly clasped hands. 'After all, why should you care what I do? It's not part of the deal.'

'Some atavistic instinct, maybe,' Alex drawled, 'connected with the word "wife". Or maybe I didn't like to think of you wasting yourself on an idiot who didn't have the wit to appreciate you the first time around. You could do better than David Sanders, Louise.'

'I'll bear that in mind,' she said, 'for the future. Is that all? May I go now?'

'Yes,' he said. 'Unless, of course, there's something you want to discuss with me?'

She hesitated. 'Has your grandmother given you any indication about the house? Her plans for it?'

'Yes,' he said. 'I'm afraid the weasely Clifford is going to be disappointed.'

'Good,' Louise said with sudden fierceness, although her heart sank within her like a stone. Her usefulness, it seemed, was at an end.

Alex grinned at her. 'How unkind of you, darling, especially when he's taken such trouble to ingratiate himself with you.'

'Not to mention the number his wife was doing on you during dinner,' Louise countered waspishly.

He laughed. 'Why, Mrs Fabian, are you implying the lady was up for it? You shock me.'

She smiled reluctantly. 'That will be the day. Now, I'd really better go and have my bath.'

She slid from under the covers and walked to the bathroom, wishing that she'd chosen a less revealing nightgown, fully aware that Alex was lying back, watching her go with undisguised appreciation.

Taking the usual unfair advantage, she thought bitterly.

As she reached the bathroom he said her name, and she looked back at him, her brows lifting in cool enquiry. Inwardly steeling herself.

'You've spent the night in my bed, and survived,' he said softly. 'So—was it really such an ordeal?'

'I don't know.' Against all the odds, Louise found her lips curving in sudden mischief. 'Luckily, I slept right through it.'

And she dodged, laughing, into the bathroom and slammed the door shut just as Alex's pillow thudded into it.

It had proved to be a day and a half, Louise thought wryly as she dressed for the party that evening.

Alex had disappeared after breakfast, having been commanded by his grandmother to take Cliff Maidstone to play golf. Della spent most of the day in a deckchair under one of the trees on the lawn, endlessly filing her nails and reading fashion magazines.

'And Louise can help me,' Lady Perrin announced regally.

This turned out to be no sinecure. Although all the arrangements for her birthday were in place, and had been for weeks, she kept having last-minute changes of plan, which Louise was detailed to relay to the staff.

But she found them placidly inured to their employer's vagaries.

'Don't worry, madam,' Mrs Gillow assured her. 'She's always liked things just so, has her ladyship, but she'll have thought again by this evening and want it all back as it was.' She sighed. 'Sad to think she's giving up the house, and this is the last party she'll have here.'

'What will happen to you and your husband?' Louise asked hesitantly. 'Will you stay on afterwards?'

'Bless you, no, madam,' Mrs Gillow said comfortably. 'Gillow and I are retiring, as planned, with a good pension that Mr Alex set up for us a while back. They've been good years here, but nothing lasts forever.'

No indeed, Louise thought sadly.

But Lady Perrin kept her too much on the run to allow time for too many recriminations or regrets.

She enjoyed the buzz engendered by the caterers and florists when they arrived, and was fascinated to see how everything came together, but secretly she found it daunting, too, and was almost relieved to know she would not be called on to organise a similar occasion at Rosshampton. No doubt it was the kind of thing Cindy Crosby would take in her stride, she thought tautly.

Alex had bathed and changed on his return from the golf course, to enable her to have all the privacy she could desire as she dressed for the party.

A long, scented bath refreshed her, and she spent time applying nail polish to her toes and fingers in the same rich red as her dress, and making up her face with extra care. The design of the dress called for nothing but a pair of ivory silk briefs beneath it, and strappy high-heeled sandals, also in red, added an elegant touch.

Louise took a deep breath, then slowly slipped the folds of gleaming taffeta over her head, and zipped them into place. Then she stood back and looked at herself in the long, old-fashioned mirror of the dressing table.

A stranger stared back at her. A girl with exotically shadowed eyes and glowing mouth, whose low-cut, tightly boned bodice cupped her small breasts like the hands of a lover. The passionate red of the dress emphasised the delicacy of her pale skin, and the graceful skirt swung like a slender bell as she moved.

For once in her life she seemed to have got it right, she thought.

There was a tap on the door, and Alex's voice said, 'May I come in?'

She took a deep breath. 'Yes—yes, of course.'

He came to a total halt as he saw her, his lips parting in a soundless whistle.

He said huskily, 'You look—very beautiful.'

He looked pretty amazing too, she thought. Black tie formality suited him. Thought it, but dared not say it.

She felt her face warming helplessly under his regard. 'Thank you, but I think we both know that's an exaggeration.' She paused. 'If you're going to tell me that your grandmother doesn't want the buffet in the dining room after all, I'm going to kill myself.'

'I've come to say that people are starting to arrive, and Selina needs us downstairs.' He produced a flat velvet case from his pocket. 'And to give you this.'

She gasped when she saw what lay on the satin bed inside. A diamond choker, with one magnificent ruby at its centre.

'It—it's wonderful. But I can't accept it.'

'You're my wife, Louise,' he told her quietly. 'I have every right to make you a gift. And you'll wear it for me tonight.'

He lifted the lovely thing from the box. 'Allow me,' he said, and fastened it round her throat.

She raised a hand and touched the gleaming stones almost with disbelief. Alex stood behind her, watching her reflection in the mirror, and she realised with shock that the hands that lightly clasped her shoulders were trembling. That in the lamplight his face looked stark, pared down to the bone. That the green eyes were suddenly hotly, broodingly intense.

The breath caught in her throat. She said hoarsely, 'I think we'd better go down. Your grandmother's waiting.'

He said, 'There's a little hook undone here on your dress.'

'I—I couldn't reach it.'

'Then I'd better.' Alex smiled at her in the mirror. 'Because it would be disastrous if this amazing creation were to slip even an inch—don't you think?'

She was beyond thought. She felt his fingers brush her naked spine, and had to bite the soft inside of her lower lip to control the small moan rising inside her.

She said, 'Yes.' And, 'Thank you.' She turned away, and picked up her evening purse, the taffeta rustling like dried leaves as she made her way to the door.

When they reached the top of the stairs Alex offered her his arm, and they descended together.

Selina, elegant in pale grey lace with pearls, was waiting in the massive hall. Beside her was Cliff Maidstone looking sullen, and Della in layers of blue tulle.

'Do you think she dyed that damned veil?' Alex muttered out of the corner of his mouth, and she was shaking with laughter, her feeling of tension evaporating fast, as they reached the foot of the stairs.

The evening became a blur of faces, young and old; some friendly, some curious. A murmur of names she would never remember, and Alex's voice saying quietly, 'This is Louise, my wife.'

When the music began Alex led his grandmother onto the dance floor, and Louise found herself partnered by a tall grey-haired man, who turned out to be the lord lieutenant of the county.

Someone else seemed to be in charge of her. Someone who smiled her acceptance each time a voice said 'May I have the pleasure of this dance, Mrs Fabian?' Who chatted animatedly with complete strangers, and ate cold salmon, and smoked chicken puffs and caviare, and drank champagne.

And who bore no relation to the shy girl caught up in a maelstrom of unfamiliar emotions, whose gaze scanned the crowded rooms for every glimpse she could garner of a tall, tawny-haired man, only to find him looking straight back at her, a smile in his eyes that set her heart pounding.

'What a nightmare,' Della muttered discontentedly at some point in the evening. 'Call this a dance? Where's the disco?'

'My grandmother doesn't like them.' Alex appeared suddenly beside them. 'Darling, I think this is our dance.'

She said breathlessly, 'Isn't there someone else you should ask?'

'I've done my duty,' he told her. 'Now it's time for pleasure.'

The music was slow and dreamy. He drew her into his arms, and they began to move to its gentle rhythm, his cheek resting against her hair. There was a space around them which gradually grew larger as people drew to the side of the floor to watch Alex Fabian dance with his new bride.

When the music ended Alex leaned forward and kissed her lightly on the cheek, then took her hand and raised it to his lips.

It was an elegant and courtly gesture, and it brought a ripple of laughter and applause from those looking on.

But his eyes, as they met hers, told Louise a very different story. They were sensuous—heavy with desire.

And they said, more plainly than any words could do, that tonight she would cease to be merely a token wife—and that he would not take 'no' for an answer.

She was trembling inside, her body suddenly weak with yearning. She was afraid too. Scared of her own inexperience, and a little ashamed too, because it was ridiculous for a grown woman to be still a virgin.

It wasn't the physical surrender she feared, anyway, but the emotional commitment. The certainty that, once taken, she would be his forever.

She stood beside him, shaking hands, saying the right, polite things as, eventually, people began to leave. She heard him decline his grandmother's offer of coffee and sandwiches when everyone had gone. And knew that there was nowhere to run—nowhere to hide.

She said her goodnights, quietly, and went with him, her hand clasped firmly in his, up to their room.

Where reality waited for her, and the possibility of heartbreak. And where the dreamlike state which had encompassed her all evening was no longer any protection.

She stood in the middle of the room, hugging herself with folded arms, as Alex removed his jacket and tie, and began to unfasten his dress shirt.

She said huskily, 'I—I need some time.'

'Take all you need,' he said. 'While I undress.'

'You're going to do that—here?'

'Yes,' he said. 'But you don't have to watch,' he added with a touch of dryness. 'It's not obligatory, and I'd hate you to be turned to stone.'

She turned away, and went across to the dressing table, her fingers nervously playing with the silver-backed mirror and the trinket boxes on its polished surface.

At last he came to stand behind her, his hands clasping her shoulders as he'd done earlier. The lamplight revealed the sheen of his skin, suggested the planes and angles of his chest, and hinted at the long, supple line of hip and thigh. She could feel the warmth of his naked body through the thin taffeta.

Her voice shook. 'Alex—please. Don't do this…'

'Do what?' he questioned. 'This?' He stroked her hair aside, and kissed the nape of her neck. 'Or this?' He bent his head and pressed his lips to her bare shoulder, forcing a shiver of response from her.

'Because I hear what you're saying, my reluctant wife,' he told her softly. 'But all evening I've seen your eyes. Felt the way you've touched me—how you went into my arms. And you know it's true.'

His fingers released the tiny hook at the back of her dress, and began to slide down the long zip.

The bodice fell away from her body like the petals of a dark red flower, baring her breasts.

For a moment she tried to cover herself with her hands, but he took her wrists and drew them gently away.

'Do you know how long I've dreamed of this?' There was a raw note in his voice. 'Of seeing you like this?' He eased the whispering taffeta down over her slender hips, and let it pool round her feet. She stepped out of it, and he picked up the mass of gleaming fabric and tossed it over the dressing stool.

He said softly, 'Now tell me you don't want me.'

His arms went round her, drawing her back against the heat of him, and she went pliantly, leaning her head on his shoulder, because her legs were shaking so that she could barely stand.

She watched herself in the mirror. Watched him as his lean fingers cupped one rounded breast, stroking gently, making the helpless breath catch in her throat, while his other hand slid down her body to curl possessively round the curve of her hip, pushing away the ephemeral protection of the ivory silk.

A stranger looked back at her. A girl with half-closed eyes, and parted rosy mouth, the erotic charge of her nakedness heightened by the blaze of diamonds at her throat, and the crimson flare of the ruby, like a drop of captured blood. A girl whose body moved restlessly under the first sensual caresses of a man's hands. Who arched against him, gasping as his straying fingers reached the shadowed cleft between her thighs. And paused.

Alex dropped to one knee beside her, undoing the strap on one sandal, then the other, and removing them. He caressed each foot, kissing the instep, then her ankle, his hands and lips moving upwards until they reached her thighs. Coaxed them apart.

His mouth was gentle, skimming over the soft skin like the brush of a butterfly's wing. Tantalising without satisfying in a way that was beyond all imagining.

She heard herself moan softly, languorously—pleadingly.

And he stood, lifting her into his arms and carrying her across the room to where the bed waited, its covers stripped away, lit by a single lamp.

Alex put her down on the mattress, and lay beside her. For a moment he was very still, looking at her, cradling her face between his hands, then his mouth sought hers with passionate, overwhelming hunger.

Louise yielded totally, her arms sliding round his neck, her fingers twining in the crisp tawny hair she'd longed so often to touch, as she tasted the sweetness of his tongue exploring her mouth.

And she returned his kiss with feverish ardour, her body melting into his, gasping as she felt the stark heat of his arousal. Pressing against him. Longing to absorb and be absorbed.

He raised his head and looked down at her, his smile crooked. 'Hey,' he whispered. 'There's no hurry, my love. I want to make this good for you. Something you'll remember.'

I'll remember, she wanted to cry out to him. Every moment of this night is going to be etched on my memory in blood—along with every word you've ever said to me, each kiss, your lightest touch.

Alex began to kiss her body, his mouth lingering on her breasts, his tongue flickering provocatively against the rosy peaks.

His hand explored gently, smoothing the slender curve of her hip bone, the slight concavity of her belly, the passage of his fingertips lighting small trails of fire in her racing blood.

Her head fell back blindly onto the pillow, her body arching up to him in mute yearning as he stroked the smooth line of her thigh, circling lightly on her flesh, pausing, then circling again, oh, so slowly. Making her wait a trembling eternity for the caress she wanted. For the intimacy of the long, clever fingers discovering the secret, molten core of her.

When he touched her, at last, as she desired, his fingers cool as they explored with exquisite precision the white heat of her need, a long, trembling sigh escaped her.

His mouth tugged on her nipples, coaxing them erect, as his fingers teased her tiny hidden bud to an equal pitch of arousal.

Deep within her, she was aware of the thrumming of a tiny pulse. Felt it strengthen—then tauten endlessly, unbearably, stretching her on some breathless rack, her senses screaming.

She made a small, stifled sound in her throat, then the tension broke, like the snapping of a wire, and her astonished body was carried away, lifted to some unknown height by wave after rippling wave of a pleasure so intense she thought she would faint—or even die of it.

And when the storm passed there were tears on her face, and Alex was kissing them away, whispering that she was his darling, his heart's delight, his beautiful, clever girl.

For a while she lay quietly, cradled in his arms, then, obeying an instinct she had never known she possessed, she moved slightly but with definite purpose, smiling up at him, her whole body a silent invitation.

He said her name softly, and slid his hands under her hips, lifting her towards him. There was no pain as he entered her. Her body was too relaxed in its own delight to offer any resistance to the smooth, fluid thrust of his possession. She was filled, completed, amazed by the reality of their union.

He paused. 'Darling.' His voice was shaken. 'Is it all right? Have I hurt you? Do you want me to stop?'

In answer, she reached up and drew him down to her, offering him the sweetness of her parted lips, and eager tongue meeting his.

He had promised her a night to remember, she thought. Well, he was going to remember it too—forever.

She caressed him in turn, running her hands over his muscled shoulders and down the strong back, forcing a smothered groan from him.

And as he began to move inside her, slowly at first, even carefully, then with increasing power, Louise found herself responding in the same way, lifting her slender legs and locking them round his hips.

Gasping, damp with sweat, she realised suddenly that her body was reacting fiercely to these new sensations, her own urgency building all over again with his, strong and inexorable. Threatening, almost before she knew it, to spiral out of control.

Knowing that Alex knew it too.

'Yes.' His voice was husky—almost fevered. 'Yes, my love—my angel.' And, 'Now.'

She felt his body convulse scaldingly in hers. Heard him call out to her. Then she was overtaken, swept away in turn, her body wrenched and shuddering in an agony of rapture.

When it was over they lay together quietly, exchanging kisses, sated and at peace.

At last, Alex propped himself up on an elbow and looked down at her, his hand gently playing with her breast.

'Well, Mrs Fabian,' he said, his voice quivering with tender amusement, 'let me congratulate you on passing your aptitude test. May I recommend you register for the advanced course?'

She stretched languorously. 'How soon does it start?'

He groaned. 'God, darling, don't tempt me.'

'You mean I could?'

He captured her straying hand and kissed it. 'Yes, you Jezebel. But it would be very selfish of me to let you.' He retrieved the covers from the floor, and arranged them round her, before pulling her back into his arms. 'You need to sleep for a while. Let your body adjust.'

'To sex?' How could anything so natural and glorious need any kind of adjustment? she wondered in bewilderment.

'No,' he told her softly. 'To having a lover. Now, rest.'

Louise wanted to say 'But I'm not tired', only it wasn't true. Her eyes were already closing, her body nestling against the warmth of his, relaxed as never before.

He whispered, 'Goodnight, my sweet.' And she felt his lips on her brow.

Yet, just before she drifted into sleep, it occurred to her with a strange, piercing clarity that he had never once said 'I love you'.

And on the heels of that came the stark and sobering realisation that he probably never would.

CHAPTER ELEVEN

THE thought stayed with her in her dreams like a dark thread in a golden tapestry, and waited for her when she awoke early the next morning.

She lay for a while, thinking. Her heart and mind might be counselling caution, but physically she was basking in a sense of well-being that she had never experienced before, while the events of the previous night unrolled in her memory in glorious, nerve-tingling detail.

She turned and looked at Alex sleeping beside her, watching the curl of his lashes on his cheek, the steady rise and fall of his chest. Then, slowly and delicately, she drew back the covers and allowed herself the indulgence of studying him in every detail.

With or without his clothes, he was heaven to the eyes, she thought, stifling a sigh, feeling the first helpless pang of desire stir anew within her. Lean, tanned all over and amazingly strong, as she'd learned last night.

She reached out a hand and touched his chest, letting her fingers stray over the flat male nipples. She bent her head and kissed them, then ran her fingers down, over his rib cage, to the firm stomach. She smoothed the clean line of his hip bone, and moved down to the long muscular thigh, where she paused, suddenly hesitant, realising that her tentative caresses were already having their powerful effect on him.

He said softly, 'Don't stop there—please.'

She withdrew her hand swiftly, helpless colour flooding her face as she wondered how long he had been lying there, observing her from under half-closed lids, that glinting smile playing round the corners of his mouth.

'So,' he went on, 'what happened to the shy lady who couldn't bear to look at me last night?'

She said, stammering a little, 'I think she died, and went to heaven.'

She paused. 'I—I didn't mean to wake you.'

'Whereas I,' he told her, 'had every intention of awakening you.' He turned onto his side, drawing her gently towards him. 'Like this,' he whispered, and began to kiss her, his lips gentle as they caressed and nibbled hers, his tongue warm and teasing as it found her own.

She yielded her mouth blindly, completely, the breath sighing in her throat as his kiss deepened, beckoned. As his fingers cupped her breast, stroking its rosy peak to renewed and almost startled awareness. Making her melt and burn with longing.

She said his name, softly, yearningly against his mouth.

He repositioned himself slightly, and without haste, raising her so that she was lying half across him, before entering her subtly and sweetly. Her breath caught, and her eyes dilated as they stared into his.

He moved gently inside her, controlling the power of his body to create a series of small, intense sensations, each one more concentrated and engrossing than the last, drawing her inexorably on.

At the same time he slid a hand down to the joining of their bodies, seeking her tiny hidden bud, brushing its tumescent heat with the tips of his fingers. Coaxing, enticing her to pleasure. Making her moan faintly, pleadingly.

Within a heartbeat, the rhythm of his body changed, became more forceful—more urgent. Taking her to some edge, holding her there for an endless moment, then releasing her into the dazzle and shimmer of a new, unguessed-at sphere of trembling, sobbing delight.

Afterwards, she lay, her face pressed into the damp wall of his chest, as she tried to recover her fragmented breathing.

When she could think, she said in a small, drowned voice, 'But you—you didn't…'

His lips touched her hair. 'I can wait.' There was a smile in his voice. 'For you.'

She raised her head, staring at him with eyes made drowsy from pleasure. 'You mean—again?'

'I hope so,' he said. 'Unless you have some objection.'

'Oh, no,' she said with a slight catch of the breath. 'None at all.'

He drew her close again, with a sigh. 'All the time we've wasted,' he said. 'All those endless days and nights when I didn't dare come near you in case you fought me off. I used to pray that you'd give some sign that you wanted me, too. Only you never did.' He shook his head. 'Even last night I was scared you might turn away from me. That you might still be hung up on that idiot you were engaged to, after all.'

She pressed her lips to his shoulder. 'You don't have to be unkind about him,' she murmured. 'I told you that David and I were never lovers.'

'I know.' His arm tightened around her. 'But I couldn't believe that he'd let you get away from him when I wanted you so badly. And when I saw him leaving the flat that day, I just lost it completely,' he added ruefully. 'Enforced celibacy clearly doesn't suit me.'

She was quiet for a moment. Then she said haltingly, 'But you haven't been—celibate, Alex. There's always been—Lucinda Crosby. I—I saw you together at that hotel. I told you so. And you didn't deny it,' she added with difficulty.

'I wasn't in the mood to confirm or deny anything,' he said with sudden harshness. 'Although I admit I should have dealt with it there and then. But I'd seen that bastard leaving, and you were there half-naked, just out of the shower. All I could think was that you'd been washing him off you, and it was driving me crazy.'

He paused. 'But if you want to talk about Cindy Crosby, we can do so now. Yes, I was seeing her at one time, and I'm not particularly proud of that. But it was over long before I met you, and I've never been even marginally tempted to resume the relationship. We're history.'

'But you were with her...'

'Briefly, yes,' he agreed. 'Because I was set up.'

'Set up?'

'Listen,' Alex said. 'I'd been approached by a guy I knew slightly who was looking for venture capital, but didn't want it generally known. He suggested lunch at the Belmayne because it was quiet and out of the way. I wasn't thrilled at the idea, because this weekend was coming up and I wanted to clear my desk, but I agreed to meet him for a drink.

'From the moment I got there, it was clear something was wrong. He was on edge, and unwilling to come to terms about his requirements, even though I'd made it plain I had no time to waste. I was just about to finish my drink and leave, when he said he had to make a phone call, and asked me to wait for him.'

He sighed harshly. 'Needless to say, he didn't come back. Instead, I was joined by Cindy, all smiles, with a table reserved in the restaurant, and a room booked on the first floor.

'I told her flatly that I wasn't interested, and that I was leaving. But she became insistent. Followed me outside. She said we'd been discreet long enough, and she wanted me back. That as long as we continued to be careful, Peter would never find out.

'I pointed out that Peter was only part of the equation. That she'd apparently overlooked the fact that I was also married now.' His voice hardened. 'She seemed to find that amusing. Told me that no one, least of all myself, could take my "ridiculous marriage" seriously.

'And that was when I walked away. In all, I was out of the bank for less than an hour, which my staff can confirm because I called back there briefly before I came home. I wanted to instruct them to take no more calls from Cindy's catspaw.'

She said with difficulty, 'Were you—in love with her?'

His mouth twisted. 'No, I haven't even that excuse. Our relationship was sexual—nothing more. A passing thing.'

He smoothed her hair back from her face with a gentle hand. 'Louise, I wasn't expecting to see her at the Belmayne. I didn't want to see her, and if you check with the barman and commissionaire at the hotel they'll tell you that our reunion was brief and unfriendly.

'But I know—none better—how easy it is to be deceived by circumstantial evidence.' He paused. 'Although I should warn you if Sanders ever comes prowling round you again, I plan to break his neck.'

She said, 'I think David came looking for comfort—needing to be told that everything would be all right. But he was disappointed. And he certainly won't be back.'

Alex bent his head and kissed her, slowly and deeply. Her response was instant and hungry, her body shivering against his. She began to touch him, her fingers exploring his bone structure and caressing his skin, trailing downwards without haste. And where her hands touched, fondled, her mouth followed, delicate at first, then moving voluptuously, all inhibitions flown.

Enjoying him in ways she had never dreamed she could. Finding, to her astonishment, that she could make him groan with need—with pleasure—in turn.

He moved suddenly, turning onto his back, his hands clasping her waist, lifting her over him, then lowering her gently onto the hard, sleek power of him.

Louise took him into her, gasping a little as he filled her, making her complete. Then she began to move on him strongly and fiercely, creating her own rhythms, her own suddenly fevered demands. He was the instrument of her pleasure, and she was his. Nothing else existed. All laughter had fled. There was no place even for words in this mutual agony of need they had created.

Louise flung her head back, arching her spine as Alex caressed her breasts, her nipples becoming pinnacles of pure sensation under the play of his fingers.

She reached culmination almost before she was aware, her voice moaning thickly at the sheer intensity of the spasms tearing through her, and heard him cry out in turn, his voice driven and anguished.

She felt herself falling, tumbling into some void, and found his arms closing round her, to hold her and keep her safe. And lying entwined with him, exhausted, she found peace, and even a kind of oblivion.

When at last Louise opened her eyes it was full daylight, and the bed beside her was empty.

She sat up slowly, fighting a ridiculous sense of disappointment, and pushed back her dishevelled hair, realising, as she did so, that she was still wearing the ruby choker from the night before. Blushing a little at the memories it evoked, she undid the clasp and put the necklace back in its velvet case on the night table.

She lay back against her pillows, stretching luxuriously, her body glowing, then tensed suddenly as there was a light tap on the door, which opened to admit Mrs Gillow, carrying a tray, which she set down on a table in front of the chaise longue.

'Good morning, madam,' she said comfortably, ignoring Louise's hasty dive under the covers. She drew back the curtains, flooding the room with sunlight. 'It's another beautiful day. Mr Alex is having breakfast with her ladyship, and asked me to bring this up for you.'

'This', Louise saw, was orange juice, a soft boiled egg, toast and tea, plus a single red rose in a small crystal vase.

'Oh,' she said, burrowing further into the bed. 'Well—thank you.' Mrs Gillow took pity on her, and fetched her robe, laying it tenderly across the foot of the bed. 'Will there be anything else, madam?'

'No.' Louise pinkened under the housekeeper's indulgent gaze. 'That's—fine.'

When she was alone, she put on the robe and trod across to the table. There was a note, she saw, propped against the vase.

'You were sleeping so peacefully, I didn't have the heart to wake you,' she read. 'But I thought your energy levels might need restoring.' And it was signed with the single initial 'A.'

The orange juice was freshly squeezed, the egg perfect, and the toast cut into neat soldiers. And she was hungry, she discovered. In fact, she was ravenous.

All the same, she wished they could have had breakfast together—on the first day of the rest of their lives. If, indeed, that was what it was. Or was she taking altogether too much for granted on the strength of one night in Alex's bed?

He'd spoken frankly about wanting her, and there was no doubt that her resolve to keep him at arm's length had simply increased his determination to possess her. And her own passionate, hidden desire for him had inevitably caused her resolution to crumble, just when she needed it most.

Well, now he'd had her, and there was no turning back. She belonged to him, helplessly and eternally, and the storm of her eventual capitulation had undoubtedly intrigued him. For a while, she could even prove a novelty for him—this token wife who'd given herself to him with such ardent lack of reserve.

But would it ever be more than that? Because she still had no idea how he viewed the future. Or what part she was expected to play in it. If any…

After all, he'd achieved his ambition, she reminded herself bleakly. Rosshampton was going to be his. She'd fulfilled the role he'd demanded, and, technically, her services were no longer required, and there was no need for the marriage to continue any longer.

Maybe the incredible pleasure he'd given her was simply a bonus, in addition to the money she'd been promised.

She winced and rose to her feet. Whatever the outcome, she told herself, it was clear they needed to talk—and soon.

She bathed and dressed in a cream linen skirt, and a sleeveless blue silky top, brushing her hair loose on her shoulders, and disguising the faintly swollen contours of her mouth with a neutral-coloured lustre.

She looked different, she thought, studying herself critically. Apart from the tell-tale shadows of fatigue, there was a new knowledge in her eyes. And a new vulnerability too.

As she walked along the gallery towards the top of the stairs, she saw Della Maidstone coming towards her, carrying a suitcase.

She checked in surprise. 'Leaving already?'

now you have to come up with the goods instead. I don't envy you the brat,' she added, winking. 'But I guess you'll have fun trying. And at least it'll be brought up in the lap of luxury. So things could be worse.'

She went down the stairs, tugging the case after her.

Louise stood rigidly at the top of the stairs, her hand clasping the banister rail so tightly that her knuckles turned white. She felt numb, paralysed with shock and hurt.

Ruthless, she thought painfully, was not the word. How long would it have been before Alex told her the real motive behind his practised seduction—if ever?

She'd wondered why he hadn't told her he loved her. Well, now she knew, and it hurt so much that she was falling apart, breaking in pieces.

She supposed he deserved credit for not having pretended to care. He'd practised a kind of honesty in that. But the fact remained that in one night she'd gone, without warning, from being a token wife to a convenient womb.

Was he really so obsessed with the place that there was no room in his life, his heart for anything else? she asked herself in anguish. It seemed so.

And that was the worst thing of all. That he was prepared for her to be just another sacrifice on the Rosshampton altar. And one that meant no more to him than Cindy Crosby had done.

For a moment she knew a flash of sympathy for the other woman, who'd found herself discarded in the cause of expediency.

She must have been desperate to pursue Alex like that, she thought. To want him back at any price. But I can't do that. I can't...

I won't plead for what he can't give. And I won't let him use me—not any more. Because I couldn't bear it.

I have to be the one who walks away. I have to...

She turned and went swiftly back to the bedroom. She fetched her case, and began filling it, throwing things in at random.

But not the red dress she'd worn last night. Or the necklace. Because she couldn't stand to see either of them again—and remember what a fool she'd been.

When the door opened behind her she tensed, instinct telling her instantly who it was, even before his hands descended on her shoulders, and his mouth grazed the side of her neck.

She stood like a statue, fighting the involuntary quiver of her senses at his touch.

'Hi,' he whispered, turning her to face him. 'I've missed you.' He dropped a light kiss on her unresponsive lips, then looked at the half-filled case.

'Packing already?' He sounded surprised. 'Gran wants us to stay for lunch, if not for another night. I think she needs to talk about the house.' He gave a faint smile. 'Convince herself that she's made the right decision.'

'Well, I'm sure you can reassure her about that,' Louise said tightly. 'If not on all points. You'd have to wait a month or two for that.'

His brows lifted. 'Is this a coded message?'

'Oh, please don't pretend.' She stepped back from him, freeing herself quite deliberately. 'Not any more. You see, it just occurred to me that we had unprotected sex last night.'

'Did we?' He was frowning suddenly. 'I thought we made love.'

'And don't play word games either,' she said raggedly. 'It amounts to the same thing.'

'No,' Alex said, 'it doesn't, but let it pass. Is there some problem?'

'Only that I could be—pregnant.'

He was very still, watching her with narrowed eyes. 'Yes,' he said, after a pause. 'I suppose it's a possibility. But would that really be so terrible?' His mouth twisted. 'After all, we're married, or had you forgotten?'

'All the same,' Louise said, trying to keep her voice steady. 'I'm wondering why you didn't take—precautions.'

'Because I had none to take.' He sounded impatient. 'I don't keep a permanent supply of condoms in my wallet in case I meet a willing lady.' He gave her a level look. 'And you've never been that, anyway, Louise. You've gone out of your way to keep me at arm's length. I had no reason to think last night would be any different.'

He paused. 'But what I need to know is—why this is suddenly such an issue. It didn't trouble you when you were weeping with pleasure in my arms. So why now?'

She shrugged defensively. 'Because last night I wasn't thinking clearly. You're very good at what you do, Alex, as you've just obliquely pointed out. Only now it's the cold light of day. And I've just realised I've taken an appalling risk.'

He was silent for a long moment. Then he said carefully, 'Are you saying you find the idea of having my child abhorrent?'

She was assailed by a sudden unwanted vision of Alex cradling a tiny, shawl-wrapped bundle in his arms, his face rapt and tender.

No, she thought, her heart contracting. *Oh, no…*

She made herself meet his gaze. Heard her voice say coolly and clearly, 'We had a deal. A baby was not part of it. You wanted the house. You have it, and if your grandmother has imposed additional conditions then that is your problem, not mine.'

He said, 'What the hell are you talking about?'

'Children.' She swallowed. 'Apparently, Selina wants them here. An extra clause in the inheritance agreement. Della warned me before she left. Or are you going to deny it?'

'I deny nothing,' Alex drawled scornfully. 'Rosshampton is a wonderful place for children, and always has been. Selina believes that, and so do I.' He paused. 'What else did Della say?'

'Just that she'd refused point-blank to become the Rosshampton brood mare.' Louise lifted her chin. 'However, I wasn't offered the same choice.'

He was very white. He said, 'Is that—truly how you see yourself? With me as visiting stud, presumably?'

She was weeping inside, but she managed a shrug. 'You said it. I didn't.'

'Yes.' He was silent again, his mouth hard and taut, his eyes studying her as if she was a stranger. 'I can't believe we're having this conversation. What happened to the warm, adorable girl I left sleeping?'

Louise shrugged defensively. 'She—woke up. Discovered reality.'

'Reality?' he repeated incredulously. 'Is that what you want? Fine.' He drew a breath. 'You feel you should have been offered a choice? Then choose now, Louise. The deal—or the marriage I thought we began last night.'

She folded her arms across her body, creating a deliberate barrier. A gesture that, she saw, was not lost on him.

He said too quietly, 'I see.' He paused. 'So, a few hours ago, you were merely on loan—is that it?'

She said stonily, 'A few hours ago I was a little crazy, but now I'm sane again, and I want my life back. All of it. As we agreed.'

He nodded, his face too expressionless, too controlled. 'What happens now, if I'm allowed to ask?'

She swallowed. 'I—I'd like to go back to London, if you'll let me have the car. I'll move out of the flat—find a hotel.'

'Try the Belmayne,' he said, his voice icily cynical. 'I hear the beds are incredible.' He paused. 'I'll have the money transferred to your account, plus a suitable bonus to compensate for my unwarranted use of your charming body.'

She bit the inside of her bottom lip so hard she tasted blood. She had the feeling that she'd thrown a stone, and started an avalanche. That events were out of control, careering away from her to ruin and despair. That if she could only turn back the clock, she would handle things very differently.

Aloud, she said, 'And if there are—consequences?'

His smile touched her shrinking flesh like the lash of a whip. 'Then deal with them in whatever way you wish, darling. And send me the bill.'

She wanted to cry out—scream in pain and negation. Instead,

she lifted her chin defiantly. 'Naturally. And now, perhaps, you'll go. Let me finish packing.'

She turned to walk past him to the wardrobe, but he halted her, his hand hard on her arm. He lifted her as if she was a featherweight, tossing her onto the bed.

'Presently,' he said. 'But first, maybe, I should give you something to remember me by.'

'Alex.' She sobbed his name as he knelt over her, his hands going to the waistband of his jeans. 'No—*please*. You couldn't...'

He paused, looking down at her, the anger draining from his face, leaving a terrible weariness in its place.

'No,' he said at last. 'Fortunately for you, I couldn't. Because I have to live with myself after this.'

His icy glance glittered with contempt. 'I wonder if you can say the same, my sweet wife.'

He went from her, leaving her lying there, staring after him, her hand pressed to her mouth.

She thought, So that's that. It's over, finished.

And then, as the pain tore through her, I've lost him. What have I done? Oh, dear God, what have I done?

It was a long time before Louise could pull herself together sufficiently to finish packing, and when there was a knock at the door she tensed, hoping—praying—that Alex had come back. But even if he had, what was there to say?

I can't stay with him as things are, she told herself wretchedly. But how am I going to live without him?

But it was only Mrs Gillow at the door to tell her that Alex's driver was waiting, and that Gillow was ready to carry her bag down to the car. She murmured a word of thanks, and fastened the bag, her hands shaking so much she could scarcely close the zip.

The hallway was deserted and the main door stood open, offering instant escape, she realised, trying to feel relieved. But as she reached the foot of the stairs Lady Perrin appeared in the doorway of the drawing room.

'Louise, my dear.' Her tone was crisp. 'I hope you were not planning to go without saying goodbye to me.'

'No, of course not,' Louise said, guiltily aware that had been her exact plan.

'Come in, then, and sit down,' Lady Perrin directed.

Louise complied with reluctance, noting that Lady Perrin had closed the drawing-room door, indicating that she had more to say than the conventional words that normally sped the departing guest.

The older woman seated herself opposite, fixing Louise with an eagle eye.

'So,' she said, 'my grandson tells me you are leaving him. That you've decided to "take the money and run", as I believe the saying is.'

Louise's lips parted in shock. She said, 'You mean—you know?'

'About that nonsensical bargain? Yes, of course.' Lady Perrin nodded. 'Alex told me all about it when he came to inform me of your marriage. He has always confided in me since he was a small child, especially when he was in trouble. And on this occasion, I had to share the blame.'

She shook her head. 'However unhappy I may have been about his way of life, his choice of companion, I had no right to interfere. And I should have realised that if I threw down the gauntlet Alex would pick it up, for good or ill.'

Louise sat up very straight. 'Was that why you decided to give him the house? Because you felt guilty that you'd pushed him into marriage?'

'Oh, no. Rosshampton was always his—if he wanted it. He knew that.'

Louise was confused. 'But what about Cliff Maidstone? He thought he was in with a chance too. Something must have given him that impression.'

Lady Perrin snorted. 'I am not responsible for that young man's delusions. He also believed that I would be fool enough to invest in some non-existent company he was touting,' she added tartly. 'I'm afraid that bad blood tells.'

She paused. 'As it did with his grandfather, of course, who was twice as good-looking, and far more charming, and with whom I briefly fancied I was in love.' She smiled reminiscently. 'You see, I was engaged to my other cousin, Alexander, whom I'd known all my life, and it all seemed very staid and settled and not particularly romantic. So Archie was a very real temptation, and it was fortunate for me that he proved far more interested in getting away with the bank's money than he was in me.'

She sighed. 'All the same, when he was sent away I was convinced my heart was broken, so my parents very wisely brought forward the date of the wedding, and I married Alexander and went on honeymoon with him.' Her face softened magically. 'And discovered with him, my dear, more passion and excitement than I had ever dreamed of. Found, in fact, that I was not merely loved, but adored, and that I could love with my whole heart in return.

'When we were together in a crowd, he used to watch me across the room in the same way that I saw Alex looking at you last night. As if I was the centre of his world—of his universe.'

She nodded. 'I knew that when my grandson found a woman to love, there would be no half-measures, and I was right. I hoped that by this time his patience might have been rewarded. And as he sat through breakfast this morning in a dream, barely hearing a word I said,' she added drily, 'I thought it had.'

Louise blushed to the roots of her hair. 'Lady Perrin,' she began.

'My dear, couldn't you call me Gran, as Alex does?'

Louise stared down at her hands, welded together in her lap. She said in a low voice, 'He doesn't love me. He married me

just to get the house. That's all it's ever been. And I can't
bear it.'

'But he doesn't have the house,' Lady Perrin told her gently.
'He gave up all claim to it when he came to see me that day.'

Louise shook her head. 'But he can't have done,' she said
in bewilderment. 'He—he wanted it so badly. He always has.'

'Once, perhaps,' the older woman agreed. 'Until he found
something he wanted far more. Until, my dear, he found you.
And, believe me, he made the sacrifice most willingly.'

'But what's going to happen to it?' Louise stared at her.
'Surely not Cliff Maidstone...'

'Certainly not,' Lady Perrin said briskly. 'At your husband's
suggestion I'm making a gift of it to a charity that helps dis-
advantaged children. He's helping me set up a trust fund to
cover the running costs.'

Louise said numbly, 'Then—*those* were the children you
meant? But Della said—Cliff Maidstone thought...'

'Yes.' Lady Perrin looked rueful. 'I'm afraid that was pure
wickedness on my part. A strong desire to see how unprinci-
pled he was—and how far he was prepared to go to achieve
his ambitions. Well, a few unguarded remarks from his wife
gave me the answer to that.' She sighed. 'But I never intended
to make mischief between you and Alex.'

'Oh, God.' Louise buried her face in her hands. 'Lady
Perrin—Gran—I said the most dreadful things to him.'

'So I gathered,' Lady Perrin said drily. 'He looked shattered
when he came to see me. And lonely, as he used to sometimes
when he was a child. I'd hoped I would never see that look in
his eyes again.'

Louise stood up. 'Where is he—please?'

'Down by the lake. I suggest you go through the French
windows and across the terrace.'

Alex was standing by the water's edge, his tall figure dark and
isolated against its glitter.

She said his name, and he turned slowly and looked at her, his face pale and deathly tired.

She said breathlessly, 'There's something I need to ask you.'

'Then will you please ask it, and go?' he said. 'As you can see, I don't take rejection well.'

She swallowed. 'Why didn't you tell me?'

He said slowly, 'There are so many things I should have told you—and didn't. Which particular one did you have in mind?'

'This house,' she said. 'Your grandmother told me you gave it up. Why, please?'

He said quietly, 'Don't you know?'

'I think so,' she said. 'I hope so. But, Alex, I need to hear you say it.'

'I gave it up,' he said, 'because I realised it would always have been a barrier between us. I wanted to be able to say to you—I want you, and only you. But if I'd accepted Rosshampton from Gran, you might always have wondered, in some corner of your mind, if I had used you. I couldn't risk that.'

'But you love it so,' Louise said urgently. 'It can't be too late. I'm sure she'd change her mind, if we went to her.'

'I don't want her to change her mind,' he said gently. 'I want us to find another house together, you and I, and make a home in it.'

'Why did you let me accuse you like that? Say those stupid, awful things to you? You could have told me the truth.'

His mouth twisted. 'Pride,' he said. 'I hated being categorised with Cliff Maidstone. And my rotten temper, which I promise I'll try to control.' He paused. 'Also, you have the power to hurt me, and make me look at myself, and ask questions as no other woman ever has. And that doesn't make me altogether rational, sometimes. I didn't know love could do that.'

'Why didn't you tell me you loved me?'

'I planned to—after breakfast,' he said. 'I was going to take you walking in the garden, your hand in mine, husband and wife stuff, and tell you that I fell in love with you when you dropped a pile of old clothes on my head, but that I didn't realise it until you came out of the house that day to drive off to Somerset.'

He shook his head. 'You were so hurt and bewildered, yet trying so hard to be brave. And I suddenly knew I wanted to pick you up in my arms and comfort you, and keep you safe forever.'

'You felt like that?' Her voice trembled.

'Oh, I had other less chivalrous impulses too.' He smiled a little. 'Like taking off your clothes and making love to you until we both fainted.'

'Suppose I'd refused to go with you that day?'

'Then I'd have become very well-acquainted with the motorway to Somerset,' he said. 'I wasn't going to let you walk out of my life. Just as if you'd left me today, I'd have come after you. You're my wife, Louise, and the only woman I'll ever want. And I shall love you until I die.'

He paused. 'Now, there's something I need to hear from you.'

She went to him then, walking into his waiting arms, feeling them fold around her. Sliding her arms round his neck to draw him down to her.

'You mean—that I love you too? Oh, darling, if you only knew how many times I've wanted to tell you.'

'I do know,' he said softly. 'None better.'

He kissed her, his mouth a tender affirmation on hers, and Louise responded, her heart on her lips.

'There is still one matter we haven't mentioned,' Alex murmured after a while. He gave her a wry look. 'You could still be pregnant.'

'Perhaps.' She smiled at him. 'But I doubt it. I think we need far more practice than that.'

'Then I suggest a swift return to London after lunch,' he said promptly. 'And an incredibly early night.'

As they turned to walk back to the house, Louise saw a movement on the water, and halted. 'Alex—look. The swans. Aren't they lovely? They've come to say goodbye.'

'Yes.' He put his arms round her as they watched the graceful birds swim majestically past them.

He said softly, 'Did you know that they mate for life?'

'How very wise of them,' Louise said, 'my dearest love.' And lifted her mouth for his kiss.

LIVE THE EMOTION

Modern Romance™
...seduction and
passion guaranteed

Tender Romance™
...love affairs that
last a lifetime

Medical Romance™
...medical drama
on the pulse

Historical Romance™
...rich, vivid and
passionate

Sensual Romance™
...sassy, sexy and
seductive

Blaze Romance™
...the temperature's
rising

27 new titles every month.

Live the emotion

MILLS & BOON®

MB3

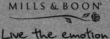

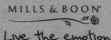

MILLS & BOON®

Live the emotion

Coming soon

PENNINGTON
Summer of the Storm

The first in a new 12 book series from bestselling author Catherine George. PENNINGTON is a charming English country town—but what secrets lie beneath?

Available from 4th July 2003

Available at most branches of WH Smith, Tesco, Martins, Borders, Eason, Sainsbury's, and most good paperback bookshops.

Live the emotion

... and get carried away with these three red-hot reads!

Miranda Lee
Caroline Anderson
Julia Byrne

MILLS & BOON

Available from 20th June 2003

*Available at most branches of WH Smith,
Tesco, Martins, Borders, Eason, Sainsbury's
and all good paperback bookshops.*

0703/024/MB77

FREE

4 BOOKS
AND A SURPRISE GIFT!

We would like to take this opportunity to thank you for reading this Mills & Boon® book by offering you the chance to take FOUR more specially selected titles from the Modern Romance™ series absolutely FREE! We're also making this offer to introduce you to the benefits of the Reader Service™ —

★ FREE home delivery   ★ FREE gifts and competitions
★ FREE monthly Newsletter   ★ Exclusive Reader Service discount
★ Books available before they're in the shops

Accepting these FREE books and gift places you under no obligation to buy; you may cancel at any time, even after receiving your free shipment. Simply complete your details below and return the entire page to the address below. *You don't even need a stamp!*

YES! Please send me 4 free Modern Romance™ books and a surprise gift. I understand that unless you hear from me, I will receive 6 superb new titles every month for just £2.60 each, postage and packing free. I am under no obligation to purchase any books and may cancel my subscription at any time. The free books and gift will be mine to keep in any case.

P3ZED

Ms/Mrs/Miss/Mr ....Initials ....

BLOCK CAPITALS PLEASE

Surname ....

Address ....

....

....Postcode ....

Send this whole page to:
UK: FREEPOST CN81, Croydon, CR9 3WZ
EIRE: PO Box 4546, Kilcock, County Kildare (stamp required)